The Fox and Dr. Shimamura

CHRISTINE WUNNICKE

The Fox &
Dr. Shimamura

translated from the German
by Philip Boehm

A NEW DIRECTIONS
PAPERBOOK ORIGINAL

The translation of this work was supported by a grant from the
Goethe-Institut in the framework of the "Books First" program.

Manufactured in the United States of America
New Directions Books are printed on acid-free paper
First published as a New Directions Paperbook Original (NDP1443) in 2019.

Library of Congress Cataloging-in-Publication Data
Names: Wunnicke, Christine, 1966– author. | Boehm, Philip, translator.
Title: The fox and Dr. Shimamura / by Christine Wunnicke ; translated
by Philip Boehm.
Other titles: Fuchs und Dr. Shimamura. English | Fox and Doctor Shimamura
Description: New York : New Directions Publications, [2019] | Originally
published as Der Fuchs und Dr. Shimamura by Berenberg Verlag in 2015.
Identifiers: LCCN 2018039751 (print) | LCCN 2018052091 (ebook) |
ISBN 9780811226257 (ebook) | ISBN 9780811226240 (alk. paper)
Classification: LCC PT2685.U56 (ebook) | LCC PT2685.U56 F8313 2019 (print) |
DDC 833/.92—dc23
LC record available at https://lccn.loc.gov/2018039751

10 9 8 7 6 5 4 3 2 1

New Directions Books are published for James Laughlin
by New Directions Publishing Corporation
80 Eighth Avenue, New York 10011

Two days ago the amphitheater at the Salpêtrière was witness to an interesting performance during Professor Charcot's characteristically crowded Tuesday Lecture. A young Japanese man, possibly a member of the folkloric troupe recently arrived in Paris, assisted the doctors with an experiment involving induced neurosis in a female patient. As soon as the woman was brought into the hypnotic state, one of Charcot's assistants led the foreign guest out from behind a screen, and his appearance alone sufficed to suggest to the somnambulatory woman that she herself was an Oriental. She invented stories, sang, and shouted in a foreign language—Charcot explained that it was Japanese and that the phenomenon required further study—and then she danced around the foreigner, weeping, begging, enticing, lamenting, all the while displaying a wide range of pantomime, in which she seemed to employ fans, daggers and all manner of exotic props, before ultimately collapsing at his feet. The effect was as touching as it was terrifying. The Asiatic guest scarcely showed any reaction. Because Charcot's assistant had led him onto the stage rather like a mannequin and shoved him back off after the experiment was over, the conjecture arose that he, too, might have been hypnotized. On account of his oriental features, which to us inevitably appear inanimate and blank, we were unable to resolve this question. We can only hope to see more of this interesting guest in the future.

—G. Demachy, *Le Temps*, March 24, 1892

The life of Dr. Shimamura was marked by tragedy. Following his return from Europe in 1894 he was scarcely active scientifically, neither in the Tokyo Medical Association nor at meetings of the neurological society. His studies on fox-possession—the first of their kind—were ignored by research. And then there was his illness. What was this illness? Despite extensive research, I have found no answer.

—Yasuo Okada, "The life of Prof. Dr. Shun'ichi Shimamura (1862–1923). A distinguished psychiatrist of misfortune," *Nihon Ishigaku Zasshi* (Journal of the Japanese Society for the History of Medicine), December, 1992

Praise be to hysteria, and to its train of young, naked women sliding along the roofs.

—André Breton, "Second Manifesto of Surrealism," 1930

The Fox and Dr. Shimamura

I

The fever came right on time, toward the end of winter. And once again Shun'ichi Shimamura, Professor Emeritus for the Treatment of Nervous Disorders, contemplated the varied paths of life. For such reflection he preferred German, and inside his brain that language spun complicated webs which gradually turned into a tangle of increasingly agitated thoughts.

Dr. Shimamura suffered from consumption. And perhaps from some additional affliction for which he could not find a suitable name in German or Japanese or Chinese or even in the gibberish of the medical professions. Inside his house in Kameoka he sat stock-still in the rattan chair between his desk and a fern set in a small metal urn with a faux patina, staring at the window, without his glasses. The late light of winter—it was the end of February, 1922—mixed with the early light of spring, giving the window paper a yellowish tinge. Perhaps his fever would soon climb so high that his mind would become completely muddled. He'd better go to bed before that happened, he thought, but only just before, since lying down is hardly a reliable antidote to life.

For a long time Shimamura had been working on a study or monograph or essay or article on the neurology or cognitive psychology or experimental psychology of memory. He had spent years arranging the chapters or paragraphs in his thoughts, and on rare occasions in a notebook, but he could never make up his mind as to the nature or scope of the text, which he had dubbed his Either/Or Project. Nor did he have a clear idea about the methodology. What he would have liked most of all was to take a galvanometric reading of the brainwaves presumably responsible for memory—ideally his own. Or at least devise some systematic classification. But he didn't own a galvanometer, and galvanometers didn't measure memory, and memory wasn't at all systematic, at least not Shimamura's. And when all was said and done he had no desire to memorize and then repeat monosyllabic gobble-dygook and wind up basking in self-importance like the late Dr. Ebbinghaus in Halle. No, what Shimamura had in mind was a prodigious and profound text about a prodigious and profound problem. Nevertheless he was certain he would die long before anything came of it, and with every passing day this certainty gave him some measure of solace. Meanwhile the Either/Or Project served as a kind of justification for passing the time recalling this and that and quite often the very opposite.

Shimamura felt a chill. With a well-practiced adjustment he shifted his body so the rattan chair wouldn't creak once he started to shiver. Over his kimono he had pulled on a well-worn burgundy housecoat patterned with fleurs-de-lis—a warm, heavy robe that bunched the kimono fabric and twisted its sleeves around his skinny arms. The doctor regularly resolved to wear the kimono on top instead of underneath, which would have fixed this annoyance, but he never did.

The housecoat was a hideous thing that Shimamura could not do without. He had bought it nearly forty years earlier in a fancy shop on Pariser Platz in Berlin, just after a storm at the height of summer, when the weather was hot and humid and not at all suited for such a plush piece of clothing. He had purchased it out of vanity: in his younger years he had liked to think of himself as mature and wise and therefore worthy of so old-fashioned a garment. Perhaps he also saw the robe as an incentive, spurring him on so that he might grow into it mentally. Above all it was an act of defiance, buying something he couldn't afford on his imperial government stipend. As he revisited those days in Berlin, Shimamura remembered having had the fever even then.

He tugged a corner of his kimono's left sleeve to free it from the heavy fabric; the hemp cloth had a beige tone that matched the window paper. Shimamura recalled a Carnival party he had attended in Vienna as Molière's Imaginary Invalid, for which he wore the same fleur-de-lis robe—at that time still brand-new—along with a sleeping cap, which turned out to be a ladies' model. He remembered becoming increasingly drunk as the night progressed, and constantly clutching a prop he had borrowed from the Bründlfeld asylum, a device for measuring tremors that was housed in an imitation snakeskin case. Girls who gave no indication if they were respectable or had just walked in off the street would finger first the case and then his robe and then the cap and then Shimamura himself. In this way he squandered an entire evening in a filthy room festooned with colored paper. Perhaps he wound up treating someone whose stomach or nerves had started to churn from all the waltzing, or maybe not. Who had invited him? Whoever it was, Shimamura now was certain that he'd been a bitter disappointment. Even as a young man on an imperial stipend, he could hardly have been described as fun-loving.

Still, he was sure he had made the girls happy, as they pranced about in their short colorful clown-puppet costumes. He always made girls and women happy. They had a weakness for Shun'ichi Shimamura—that was a chapter of his memory all to itself. Although "weakness" wasn't quite the right word and probably neither was "happy."

Shimamura took one of his nearly blank notebooks out of the desk drawer and stuck it in the pocket of his robe, alongside his handkerchiefs and the tiny vial of camphor.

Dr. Shimamura had four nurses: Sachiko his wife, Yukiko her mother, Hanako his own mother, and a maidservant he sometimes called Anna but more often Luise. He had brought her along when he retired from the Kyoto asylum, as a kind of memento, and because no one there knew for sure whether she was a patient or one of the nurses. In fact no one could remember her name. That made Shimamura feel sorry. As the director of the clinic he had been known for his soft heart, his constant concern that no one would get hurt, that no one's suffering would go unconsoled, and that all examinations were performed without causing undue aggravation. He arranged to have female nurses stationed in the men's asylum, because they exuded calm, and he was unstinting in his use of hypnosis. On top of that he commissioned a mat weaver to make special padding for the walls of the more agitated patients' rooms. These special mats, which Shimamura had invented, were mentioned at his retirement ceremony more than any other accomplishment—which was rather disappointing after an entire lifetime devoted to medicine.

Tucked away in Kameoka, where he wasn't a "bother" as he put it, to anyone, and where by now he had spent years waiting for his death, he had ordered similar padding for two walls he had had constructed out of plaster, wood and a little stone to isolate his room from the rest of the house. One of these walls contained a European door with a brass handle. According to the workers who had executed his design, the walls compromised the integrity of the entire building. They also failed to shield him from the four women, who clattered about at four separate places inside the house while he sat in his rattan chair next to the desk staring at the window, and now at any moment three of them would come striding through the door to check on him.

By this time Hanako and Yukiko were both well over eighty. While Hanako was lanky and asthenic like her son, Yukiko was soft and round. She was also more relaxed, and took each day as it came. Through years of shared caring for the doctor their voices had grown so much alike that sometimes Shimamura couldn't tell which ones were whispering behind the door. Frequently his dreams fused them into a single mother figure that expanded and contracted like some smoky apparition out of a fairy tale. Now and then Yukiko visited the temple where she made a small monetary offering, after which she would come back in a cheerful mood. Hanako read modern novels, mostly by female authors, which dealt discreetly with various family problems. What Yukiko and Hanako felt for each other, whether it might be hate, love, solidarity, competition or simply that dull, comfortable resentment that results from people living together for too long, Shimamura couldn't say. His sickness was the sun they orbited around, and which provided them warmth. One of them had said as much to him once, and for that reason Shimamura hated them both.

He had been married to Sachiko for thirty-one years. She hovered between the two mothers like a specter, unobtrusive and inconspicuous but nonetheless commanding. She wore nothing but light-colored clothes, even in winter, always perfectly creased in just the right places. When Shimamura looked for adjectives to describe his wife, the first words that inevitably sprang to mind were "prismatic" and "crystalline"—inorganic chemistry. Seemingly immune to Dr. Shimamura's special attraction for women, she evidently possessed substantial, if not exactly pleasant, willpower.

Hanako brought food and Yukiko brought tea. Sachiko made certain she was in the room before the mothers so she could observe their doings, after which she observed her husband, how he drank, ate, and coughed, as well as the way he prepared the scopolamine injection he was now permitting himself after three days of abstinence. Then Hanako and Yukiko cleaned up as Sachiko moved soundlessly through the room, while Anna or Luise lurked behind the door, taking whatever she was handed: teacups, plates and bowls, a handkerchief to be laundered. Although his meal had consisted of rice balls and pickled vegetables, Shimamura—who couldn't think of anything else to say—repeated the doctors' tired joke about restorative soups, that they should be just like a young girl, lean and wholesome. In Japanese the joke sounded absurd, even lewd, as though eating had somehow triggered the patient to babble about young women. Shimamura thought he saw Sachiko cast a concerned glance at the scopolamine injection he was holding.

Scopolamine did indeed stimulate thoughts of a sexual nature, which might be detrimental in the treatment of nervous disorders, but this did not trouble Shimamura when it came to medicating himself. Besides, at this stage he no longer trusted his brain anyway, so it might as well focus on sex. What did trouble him were the four women. They seemed to him like pieces of a tile game—big triangle, little triangle, diamond, square—that were forever forming new combinations, a never-ending and pointless way of passing the time. "Go and amuse yourselves," he told them. "See if it's already spring outside. And please tear February off the calendar."

Then they were gone. Only Anna or Luise was still hovering by the door. Shimamura could hear her quiet, flat footsteps. She walked with the wide, outward-bearing gait indicative of deficient hip stabilization. The woman had many defects, but Shimamura couldn't determine which one was primary. Every morning she brought a whole bucketful of water to his bed. Shimamura didn't know who had told her to do that, or what he was supposed to do with all the water, or whether it was merely a misunderstanding and Luise actually meant to bring the inhaler when she came waddling in on her duck-like feet.

He accepted the water with an annoyed smile, whereupon Anna-Luise gave an overly deep bow before scooting away. Now and then Shimamura was convinced she ran off every day to some safe place, perhaps to the toilet or else an open field, where she could relapse into insanity, into some disorder of unclear origin that had afflicted her at least since Kyoto and had never been treated, symptomized by loud, forceful and possibly obscene outbursts, after which she rested for ten minutes or maybe even a solid hour and then waddled back as though nothing had happened, with the gentlest hint of satisfaction on her farm girl's face. If he had only caught her once while she was raving, Shimamura thought to himself, he might have been able to heal her, and she would be free to go and lead a healthy female life instead of vegetating here.

I'd like to have these stupid walls torn back down, Shimamura thought, so I can die in a normal house. Then he injected the scopolamine into his thigh and went to bed.

Not one single sexual thought came to entertain him that afternoon. His brain simply kept repeating: calendar, calendar, February, February, calendar, calendar... Then it started asking questions: where is the gramophone, where could the inhaler have disappeared to, what happened to the German Charcot and why is the bookcase filled with whole yards of Charcot in French even though no one here understands that language? And what had become of all his good clothes? The European as well as the Japanese? Did the women toss them in the oven because it's clear I have no more use for them? And where are Father's heirlooms, for instance the second-rate calligraphy with the large and simple characters and the life maxims no one could possibly live up to? All gone, said Shimamura to his brain, let it be. And suddenly he saw his father's calligraphies and was unable to read them because he was only seven years old.

"*Als ich klein war*," he said, in German — "When I was little." He sighed once and then again. The air went in and out. That was pleasant. The injection did him good. To calm his bronchia he was happy to look at the large characters with seven-year-old eyes and feel helpless in the face of their silent reprimand. Or sense his five-year-old ears being cleaned by his mother's hands, in a golden hundred-year summer with a golden sun that caused his fingers to glow red when he held them up to his eyes. He happily accepted all the cicadas and the ghosts and the windmills, and the windmill ghosts and the outhouse ghosts who were after his bare bottom, which he showed publically everywhere because his country still lived in the Stone Age. Pff, said Shimamura, and he let the phantom of the bamboo ear pick awaken the old feelings lurking within, as if something were pushing into his head and cleaning it out because he was all muddled on the inside.

Shimamura stared at the ceiling.

The women. The women. The women?

Not a single sexual thought came to his assistance.

The women and myself. What happened?

Kitsune-tsuki, he said — fox-demon possession.

He laughed the little laugh reserved for this word. Then he fell asleep.

2

"Everyone has the same memories from childhood, Sensei,"
declared the student. "We all remember the way our mother
cleaned our ears, and the windmills, and the noises in the
night."

The student was walking two steps behind Dr. Shimamura, along a barely visible path between the rocks and
the undergrowth. It was a hot summer day in the Shimane
prefecture—July, 1891, according to the new calendar. Young
Dr. Shimamura had recently completed his studies in Tokyo,
where he had been the favorite pupil of Hajime Sakaki, professor of psychiatry.

"Please," the student insisted, "don't you agree, Sensei?"

Shimamura didn't answer. He was long used to the student's
chatter, whose impoliteness bordered on mental aberration.
What was his name? Surely Shimamura had known at one
time, but later he forgot it, in fact it was astounding how completely he'd blocked it from his memory. And even back then
he had never used it, but only referred to him as "student."

They clambered through the underbrush. Shimamura carried his medical bag with stethoscope, gynecological speculum, Helmholtz ophthalmoscope, reflex hammer and Wilhelm Griesinger's *Mental Pathology*, third edition, while the student lugged a large English duffle bag full of camera equipment. Shimamura wore a Norfolk jacket, straw hat and button boots. The student meanwhile had a loose peasant tunic that came down to just above the knees, and straw sandals that flapped as he walked.

"Do you also remember, Sensei, being told when you were little that if you left one shoe by itself it would turn into a shoe-ghost and come after you?" asked the student.

Three days earlier, in a moment of desperation, Shimamura had told him to borrow some local clothes and put them on, claiming this would help win the trust of the rural population. In truth he hoped that such undignified dress might put an end to the student's babbling, but that didn't happen. Now Shimamura was envious of all the air reaching the student's body, especially around the neck. Shimamura's own collar chafed and was so tight that whenever he turned his head he could feel his carotid pulse, and beads of sweat lined his slender moustache.

"And yet if everyone has the same childhood memories, isn't it astounding that we all turn out so different?" the student declared triumphantly.

Shimamura had no idea why Professor Sakaki had made him take as his assistant this particular medical student, who was probably no more than fifteen or sixteen years old. Nor could he say what the professor actually hoped to achieve with the entire expedition. "Go to Shimane," Sakaki-sensei had said, "and study the annual epidemic of *kitsune-tsuki*. Examine every single afflicted woman and make a diagnosis. Pay particular attention to symptoms suggestive of nervous disorders." So now Shimamura had spent days traipsing through the most miserable and forlorn districts of Shimane, where he'd examined a number of pitiful women said to be possessed by the fox demon, and had diagnosed the most annoying diseases (dipsomania, cretinism, an ovarian abscess rupturing into the rectum)—but he still had no idea what kind of trick Professor Sakaki was playing on him. "If no diagnosis is forthcoming," his mentor had instructed, "then just write down 'Fox' hahaha." Sakaki-sensei liked to joke. Perhaps the whole expedition was simply one big joke on the part of his professor.

The journey from Tokyo to Shimane took nearly two weeks. On foot. By litter carrier. In rickshaws with the student practically on his lap and constantly jabbering away. He was the scion of an ancient house whose family tree was worthy of awe. There were grandfathers and great uncles and great aunts who had died of eccentric, archaic diseases as soon as Japan opened its borders. There was also a four-hundred-year old war fan which one of the student's ancestors had raised at the wrong moment, thereby causing the battle to be lost. The fan was preserved in the family shrine, a four hundred-year-old reminder of the value of humility. For two weeks the young student had related every single detail to Shun'ichi Shimamura in various rickshaws and inns, all the while smoking his pipe. Moreover, unlike Shimamura, he knew a lot about foxes. He counted the fox goddess Inari among his ancestors, and undoubtedly innumerable superstitious traditions had been passed down as family lore. He knew cases of fox possession stretching back four centuries, all of which befell the vassals of his powerful family. These, too, he related in great detail.

At home in Tokyo, Shimamura had worked on paralytic beri-beri and hereditary melancholia. He had been preparing for his trip to Europe which would take place as soon as he was granted an imperial stipend. He had also just gotten married to a doctor's daughter, an unfriendly beanpole of a girl he couldn't figure out. The young Shun'ichi Shimamura understood as much about women as he did about foxes. Nor did he fare particularly well with them, his female patients included. He was happy to report that the fair sex remained for the most part unafflicted by hereditary melancholy and paralytic beri-beri. Of course it was entirely possible that Sachiko, whom he had to marry because he was Professor Sakaki's favorite student, was not so unfriendly by nature, but only around him. Was this perhaps the point of the professor's practical joke? Meanwhile the student kept delivering the same lecture day in and day out: "It's not a fox, Sensei, it's a vixen! From woman to woman. All firmly in female hands!" Was Sakaki-sensei sitting in the Imperial University in Tokyo at his magnificent English desk beside the small statue of Hygieia merrily laughing up his sleeve because, of all people, Shun'ichi Shimamura was spending weeks in the scorching heat doing nothing but examining old-fashioned female insanity—with no benefit to science whatsoever?

"Would you just keep your mouth shut for once," Shimamura told the student, who hadn't actually been saying anything. Shimamura tripped over a dry root and stubbed his toes. "Over there's a shady spot, Sensei," the student proclaimed, pointing to the thin trunk of a thin tree with very few leaves. The student thrived and flourished in the heat. Shimamura suffered from low blood pressure and the summer dyspepsia that asthenics are prone to. He gratefully took advantage of the tiny bit of shade, where he squatted for a moment and closed his eyes. Then he studied the hand-drawn map provided by the director of the Matsue hospital, which for years had been responsible for Shimane women afflicted by fox-possession.

That day's work focused on an area between Taotsu and Saiwa, where the director had marked three red fox signs, indicating that the fox had nested there three times. The unnamed location wasn't very far, so Shimamura took a deep breath, squeezed his buttocks together to stabilize his blood pressure, and set off again.

On the way they were dogged by half-naked children scurrying out from under every rock and bush. Many carried smaller siblings on their backs, who slept or slobbered or chewed their little fists. They were probably all suffering from malnutrition of some sort. Whenever Shimamura glanced in their direction they scattered like a school of fish. The children showed no respect for the student, creeping up and tugging at him—and it wasn't long before the first were clinging to him like barnacles to a boat. The student made faces at them. In his threadbare tunic he looked like their big brother. To shield his head from the sun he had tied on an old rag that made a mockery of any concept of hygiene. Despite all his annoying ways, the student was a good boy. Shimamura resolved to pay him a little more attention and perhaps teach him a thing or two about medicine, as long as the youth was in his charge.

They arrived at Taotsu, which they crossed in five minutes before again finding themselves in the pathless and pointless heat. By now the exorcists had joined the children; every day it was the same game. They, too, avoided Shimamura and worked on the student instead. There were already four of them: a limping monk, a little woman with magical banners, and two "receptacles."

"Two receptacles have just joined us, Sensei!" the student announced with scarcely concealed enthusiasm.

The student knew how badly the so-called receptacles disgusted Shimamura, and Shimamura was not one to be easily disgusted—after all, he was a doctor. Only yesterday he had abraded several skin lesions on a leprous female, simply as a respite from all the fox-women. But Shimamura really did feel a tremendous aversion toward the receptacles, and now he turned around and yelled. He screamed at the children and at the exorcists. He raised his fists, threatened to call the police, brandished his syringes—all to no avail. The children and exorcists made a big show of leaving only to sneak right back. And so it went day after day. Already the first receptacle was peeking over the student's shoulder. "Shove off!" Shimamura bellowed. He felt a shiver despite the heat.

The so-called receptacles were the most pathetic exploiters of the fox-madness, and to group them with the exorcists would be an insult to the latter. The hospital director in Matsue had explained it all exactly. Every summer the most desperate lowlifes made the pilgrimage to Shimane to offer themselves as *fox-receptacles*. As *fox-shelters*. As *fox-asylums*.

There were many names and each one was disgusting. The short form "receptacle" disgusted Shimamura the most. The ones who came to Shimane all wore a leash around the neck. Like a dog. Or a donkey. The leash said: Take me, I am your sacrifice. Oh how they filled Shimamura with loathing! When the fox demon left a possessed person—so Shimamura had learned—it was important not to leave him floating around homeless, and the receptacles made sure he had another place to go. They held soft tofu in their open mouths in order to attract the fox, the fox would come and sniff and lick and take the bait, and then would get swallowed—always with a lot of roaring and wrenching about. The hospital director described this transfer to Shimamura in great detail; just like the student, he enjoyed seeing how much the whole thing disgusted the know-it-all from Tokyo. The director also described what happened next to the receptacle or shelter or asylum: once the fox was inside, the receptacle succumbed to a puny, whimpering, drawn-out insanity and a very slow death characterized by a distinct odor. "We happen to have one lying out back. Don't you want to have a look?" A special prayer was said over the body of the receptacle, in which the fox demon was now securely—or perhaps insecurely—enclosed, then the corpse was quickly tossed onto a weed fire or into the sea or a river or perhaps somewhere near a well with drinking water. (Dr. Shimamura came up with the last idea, as well as with the notion that particularly strong receptacles could accommodate several foxes before bloating up and ultimately exploding. By then he was dreaming of the receptacles, and in greater and greater detail, so deep was his disgust.)

Both of today's receptacles, he ascertained, one male and

one female, had surreptitiously untied their leashes, so the man in the straw hat wouldn't guess their office. Now they walked sanctimoniously alongside the monk. Even they knew of Dr. Shimamura's loathing and were taunting him.

Shimamura found himself searching for stones fit for throwing.

"There, up ahead!" the student shouted out in glee as he gave his pipe a triumphant knock to dump the ash.

The three red marks on the map were easy to spot in real life: well over a dozen receptacles were standing, lolling, sitting, and lying amid a whole forest of magical banners surrounding two huts so low they could have been stalls.

"May I take a photograph please, Sensei?" the student called out.

Shimamura fought to keep down the juices churning in his stomach.

"No, thank you," said Dr. Shimamura. "As I have already explained to you we are conducting medical research, not ethnographic studies."

The three fox signs marked by the hospital director from Matsue turned out to be an epileptic who fortunately presented a classic Jacksonian seizure within the first five minutes, her malingering sister, and an imbecilic neighbor who showed no other symptoms than her imbecility. The student was allowed to photograph the epileptic, but that didn't satisfy him, since it was too dark inside the foul-smelling hut, and of course the seizure was long gone. So he proceeded to photograph the malingering sister as well as the imbecilic neighbor, albeit without first asking permission. He moved them both into the sunlight and had them pose in front of the banners, while Shimamura tried with great effort to coax a case history of the Jacksonian patient from her pitiful mother.

As always, Shimamura was unable to make any specific findings in the cases of alleged possession. As always, he was unable to follow the whining and whimpering of the country folk. And as always, the patients screamed bloody murder as soon as he attempted to examine them, and then, still howling, threw themselves on the student without restraint.

Along with the photography, receiving these desperate embraces had become the student's second hobby. He wore the imprint of the filthy, tear-ridden girls' faces on his chest like a ceremonial sash. Who could say if one of his accursed ancestors hadn't laid healing hands on some lowly serfs four hundred years ago, and that perhaps some of that talent had been passed down to him. What's more, he would whisper back and forth with all the sick people and their relatives — and clearly nothing concerning modern medicine. Once he went so far as to let a poor woman with an ovarian abscess spit on his hand, and then put on an earnest show of carrying it outside; Shimamura had watched him do it. He hadn't questioned the student's actions: he was too taken aback to forbid the young man such lunacy. But afterwards he lost three nights' sleep wondering whether the student had paid one of the receptacles lurking outside to swallow the poor woman's spittle. There was no doubt that the student was blithely offering his services as an exorcist, and Shimamura didn't want to know anything about it. Inside the dark shack somewhere between Taotsu and Saiwa, where — instead of wiping away the urine the epileptic woman had abundantly dispensed — everyone was fervently praying, Shimamura came to the conclusion that he found all of it disgusting—the diseases, the people, medical science and superstition and the foxes and even Dr. Griesinger's mental pathology.

For two weeks Shimamura and his student trekked across the scorching Shimane prefecture. There was no lack of foxes, but none of the patients displayed neurological symptoms, and even the psychiatric diagnoses remained vague. After many cases of tuberculosis, one of meningitis, three simple flus and all manner of nonspecific paralytic disorders, Shimamura had had enough and with no real justification he diagnosed one case of choreatic mania, simply because he liked the sound of the words, as well as one of gravidity psychosis.

Most of the people had nothing wrong with them. And while Shimamura looked the other way, the student healed them in his usual manner.

After two weeks Dr. Shimamura's own condition had grown into full-blown neuro-asthenia, and his dyspepsia had become so explosive that for one whole day he thought he'd contracted cholera. The student had long since stopped following him on the paths and instead marched proudly in front, bending branches out of his master's way and shooing off the receptacles so Shimamura wouldn't have to. In the meantime he talked. And laughed. And smoked. And sang. Shimamura felt as though he'd grown old while the student had simply grown up, having matured into a man—although one clearly ill-served by German medical teachings. Shimamura had long ago given up teaching him anything. He couldn't understand the student's old songs any better than he could the fox patients' moaning and groaning. Finally he decided to turn back.

"Now that you've done your duty exploring the rabble," said the Matsue hospital director, when Shimamura tried to leave, "it's time for you to see our little lady. Here you go. A new map. I've been saving her for last, just for you. Right here …" and he pointed to an enormous blood-red fox surrounded by a halo, emblazoned on a remote location beside a steep cliff. "Here you will find the blessed fishmonger's daughter. Our celebrity. Your reward. The fox princess of Shimane."

3

By Friday the weather was perfectly beautiful and since his fever hadn't risen, Dr. Shimamura went for a walk with his wife.

Sachiko had never acquired a taste for this activity, even after so many years. She didn't see the sense in running around outside for the sake of one's health instead of lying in bed and sparing one's strength, which of course was already depleted if one was sick. Even in Kyoto she had always felt a little insulted whenever her husband extolled the benefits of fresh air: as if her own house had a bad smell—as if one had to resort to outdoor public spaces to clear the lungs. On occasion, when there was too much talk of walks, she set out enormous bouquets of flowers. Shimamura had never understood this silent criticism.

Sachiko Shimamura strode alongside her husband with an austere expression and a folded umbrella. There was nothing to see. It was too late for snow and too early for flowers and the castle was far too far away. Of course the temple did have a beautiful garden, but ever since Yukiko had taken to paying to get in, just so she could touch the miracle-working statue, the Shimamuras felt embarrassed and went out of their way to avoid the temple. The river wasn't particularly beautiful, and it was almost as far as the castle. So the only thing left was a purposeless stroll. Sachiko cautiously placed her feet on the path that led from their somewhat remote house through the fields in the direction of town. With every third step she moved the umbrella forward, in an effort to conjure some concrete feeling along the way. After a while she managed to create a kind of rhythm that disposed of the seconds in an orderly manner, and she gave up her resistance. At least it isn't raining, she thought, there's no one coming we have to greet, and it is February, after all.

Shimamura mumbled something incomprehensible. She didn't bother to ask, since it was undoubtedly a variation on the statement "the yields around here could definitely be improved." He always said that when he took the path between the fields. All his life he'd spent his free moments thinking about important matters, without ever putting his thoughts into practice, and agronomy was one example. "Yes, dear," said Sachiko.

At nearly sixty years she still stood very upright and proud. And she was tall, too, with a long neck and long arms she never let dangle alongside her body but always held neat and proper. She didn't like having empty hands—hence the umbrella. Sachiko resembled her husband and her mother-in-law more than she did her own mother. When their families arranged the marriage this had been a constant theme: how well suited in height the bride and groom were. The fact is that no one could think of anything else to say. Sachiko wasn't exactly dying to marry the young doctor. He seemed nervous and constantly engrossed in thought and during two weeks of courtship managed to break his glasses twice. She didn't like that, but there were no significant objections and so she didn't refuse.

Like her husband, Sachiko was inclined toward contemplation, though this wasn't evident at first glance, as it was with him. Even romantic notions weren't completely alien to her; as a girl she had dreamed of having long white wings instead of long white arms, of flying away and abandoning all reason, to find passionate love in the arms of some man who was not a doctor and had no doctors in the family. But that fantasy was long ago, and all that remained of it was a preference for light colors. She wore a light-colored headscarf and a light-colored shawl around her light-colored house dress. A bit of gray hair peeked out from under her headscarf. Sachiko hoped it would turn entirely white once she became a widow.

Sachiko often ruminated for long periods and in great detail about her widowhood.

"Another letter arrived about the woodcuts," said Sachiko. "A German from Tokyo. He wants to take the train out here to have a look. Also a colleague wrote about the wall padding—but no one you know."

Shimamura furrowed his brow and surveyed the poorly yielding fields of Kameoka. Then he muttered a scarcely audible "hmm" and returned to his thoughts, as Sachiko knew without having to turn her head.

"*Abschmettern?*" Sachiko asked in German if she should throw the letters out.

This elicited another, slightly more spirited "hmm."

For years this *abschmettern* comprised one of Sachiko's many duties in Kameoka. She opened her husband's correspondence and if it wasn't one of his three friends—all doctors, two in Kyoto and one in Heidelberg—she would read the letter from beginning to end and either ask pro forma or not at all, and then *abschmettern* into the waste basket. German had such ugly words. Sometimes, although more and more seldom, she imagined herself traveling to Germany as a tourist, perhaps to see the Starnberger See, and trying to converse with a local. *Abschmettern. Schnupftuch. Intravenös. Türklinke. Psychopathologie.* What a short and silly conversation that would be. And just then she felt such a flood of ennui as the world had never known. It took her breath away for a moment and threw her out of step. She stared blankly at the fields. Up at the sky. Over to her husband. Back to the sky. And down at her toes in their white stockings. Then she said *"ach ja,"* and counted out nine steps and three umbrella thrusts. And the ennui shrank from an earth-shattering phenomenon into ordinary boredom.

"The German was very keen on seeing your woodcut collection," Sachiko said.

Shimamura didn't react, and Sachiko did not persist. As it was, both letters were her own invention. Since fewer and fewer arrived, she invented some at regular intervals, to bolster Shimamura's will to live. Sachiko believed that as long as one is receiving mail from someone who can be consigned to *abschmettern*, then one can still feel a sense of belonging to the world. And any mention of padding or woodcuts was bound to bother Shimamura. He was annoyed at being known solely for psychiatric wall padding and a collection of fox woodcuts. As long as a person gets annoyed, thought Sachiko, that person won't die. And a nurse had a duty to delay the death of any person under her care. This seemed like a platitude, but one she needed to remind herself of now and then.

"*Ach ja,*" said Shun'ichi Shimamura.

"Shall we head back?"

"After the curve."

As always they continued past the curve. Then they slowly made their way back home. A cloud passed in front of the sun. Shimamura's breathing became more labored. Sachiko felt a twinge of conscience as she recalled the one letter she had never told her husband about. The one she kept hidden under the floor of the south room, inside a pharmacology manual that had belonged to her father. It was from someone wanting to purchase Shimamura's entire woodcut collection—the man had even named a price, and a good one at that. Sachiko would write back after her husband had died, so that all those foxes wouldn't be a millstone around her neck when she became a widow.

Halfway to their house, by the quince trees, they saw someone out and about and they stopped. The Shimamuras greeted their neighbors only grudgingly. But it was just the maidservant. She was standing among the bare quince trees, singing:

> *In the tall grass, in the short grass*
> *In Uji and Kei*

My beloved insisted and he had his way
Oh grandmother please oh won't you soon die
Or we'll have no choice but to all starve away

And then she began all over again.

Shimamura stood still and listened. And he smiled, like he was hearing the first spring bird or some other beautiful thing. Sachiko didn't look at her husband, he had actually stepped a bit behind her, as though seeking protection, but she could feel his smile nevertheless.

The girl had a strong voice, yet her singing sounded constrained, as if her mouth was closed, and she was gripping the trunk of a quince tree with both hands. She hadn't seen the Shimamuras. Her song was desperate, but also artful, with all kinds of tremolo. Sachiko kicked a little stone, but the stone was too small, as was Sachiko's kick, and the girl began her song for the third time, with variations, as though she were all alone in the world. Shimamura kept smiling behind Sachiko's shoulder. His breathing was easier now.

"I remember that song," he whispered. The girl gave a start and let go of the tree, restrained her stubborn voice with effort, said "grandmother" in a trembling voice, and ran off.

"There is no such song," said Sachiko. "There's no song with 'Uji and Kei.'"

"She got scared and ran off," said Shimamura. "My mother or your mother used to sing this song. Or someone else. I still know the words."

"By the way you shouldn't call her Luise," said Sachiko. "She can't pronounce that. She runs around all day mumbling Luise, Luise, until she's worn herself out. And your mother never sang a song with 'Uji and Kei' and my mother didn't either. There's no song in the world with 'Uji and Kei.'" You aren't remembering correctly. And her name isn't Luise. Poor thing!"

Sachiko had suddenly raised her voice. Shimamura took another step back and stared at her, flabbergasted. He looks so miserable, Sachiko thought, just standing around here. She reached for her headscarf and tucked her hair inside.

"I mostly call her Anna …" Shimamura muttered.

Back then, when she had simply taken the girl from the Kyoto asylum and brought her to Kameoka, so that her husband might show a little more desire to live, Sachiko had completely overlooked the fact that the girl was such a poor thing.

"Shall we go home, dear?"

"Hmm."

They took another moment to enjoy the weather, which really was very nice for February, and then made their way home.

4

Ever since he caught the housemaid—whose name he could no longer remember—ever since he caught her singing by the quince trees, Dr. Shimamura, or really Dr. Shimamura's brain—as he occasionally said when he didn't want to use the word "I"—was convinced that the song with Uji and Kei came from the Shimane fishmonger's daughter Kiyo.

There was nothing odd about that: Shimamura's brain manufactured many memories he couldn't place. These he attributed to Kiyo, and he was powerless against them. It was Kiyo who had inspired the Either/Or Project. She was the besetting issue for his psychology of memory, the pivotal point in his own medical history. She was also the reason he wound up in Vienna, where her case quickly became the gossip of unkind colleagues .

Dr. Shimamura took his temperature. Afterwards he listened to make sure no one was coming, that the women were all well out of the way, and pulled a few volumes of the French Charcot off the shelf. He then reached further back and fished out the small bundle containing the evidence from Kiyo's case. Little girl's toys, a stuffed monkey on a bamboo stick, a shuttlecock, a spinning top, paper flowers. Occasionally Shimamura had the feeling that these odds and ends were all he remembered of Kiyo, and that the only reason he could remember them was because he could hold them in his hands whenever he wanted. He fingered each object and then packed everything back away. The toys were bitten and chewed as though they had belonged to a dog.

The fishmonger's house lay in a shady mountain hollow high above the sea. It was a beautiful home, almost princely. Here the fish weren't wares to be hawked but inventory that was managed in lucrative fashion, and the fishmonger, as it turned out, was a prince among fishmongers, although Shimamura and the student never learned how that had come about, or why fish and their management were so greatly valued there.

The climb had been taxing, and the young student had repeatedly rendered yeoman service. He found natural footholds in the stone for the exhausted neurologist, and once even saved the older man from falling—out of fatigue and also from a kind of despair—off a cliff.

No exorcists or receptacles were loitering beside the steep bank. No children followed them. It was very quiet, very hot. Here and there a plucked bit of white could be seen hanging in the branches—tufts or fur from something scampering by. Now and then they felt a light air, and Shimamura would take off his hat to cool his head, but it wasn't a sea breeze, it was a waft of something sticky and stifling, almost like smoke from something burnt.

"Do you remember when we were little," the student asked, "how we always had to leave out the number four whenever we counted, because it summons death? One, two, three, five, six, seven? Do you remember, Sensei?"

The student was wearing only a loincloth. The peasant tunic which the fox patients had been snatching at for two weeks was now completely in tatters, and the young man had wrapped it around his head, so that the sleeves flapped down over his ears onto his shoulders. Shimamura said nothing as he watched the man's naked bottom dance through the scrub brush on top of the cliff. The student was now carrying Shimamura's medicine bag in addition to the photographic apparatus. Shimamura took off his hat and put it on again. A dragonfly went purring by. Shimamura remembered the number four and the god of death. He felt himself succumbing to fear—to an old, ancient fear.

The wealthy fishmonger did not live in his beautiful home. Perhaps he'd never lived there. Perhaps he'd only built it to house his possessed child along with her mother, a few aunts, and a number of maids and caretakers, and then run off somewhere. Shimamura and the student never found that out, either.

Dr. Shimamura had set aside one hour for his final assessment. Instead it went on for two and a half weeks. And during all that time his calendar, where he kept a daily log for Professor Sakaki, showed not a single entry: for the days spent with the girl Kiyo it was completely blank.

Her guardians made the doctor wait a long time before taking him to see the patient, who looked to be about sixteen. A blossoming beauty, with long hair done up in a pile of twists. She was sitting by herself at a small table in a large room flooded with sunlight, her legs crossed, playing with a tattered magazine called *La Vie Parisienne*.

"Sensei!" she called out to Shimamura's silence. "I beg your pardon!" The magazine slipped from her hands as she stepped in front of the table and sank to her knee in a deep bow.

Because he didn't know the most appropriate response, Shimamura, too, knelt down, keeping a far greater distance than called for. He regretted he'd been so ashamed of the naked student that he had confined him to the garden instead of bringing him inside. Still bowing deeply and without moving, Kiyo peered vaguely at Shimamura through her eyelashes and a loose strand of hair. Sakaki must have pulled her from some theater, he thought, she's really the young diva of a highly modern female troupe from Tokyo, and Professor Sakaki sent her to Shimane just to irritate me. Half-bent and wholly cramped, he observed his new patient, while wondering whether he himself wasn't displaying some paranoid tendencies he'd never noticed before.

Kiyo's back began to rise and fall. Her breathing grew deeper, then faster. And faster. Pumping like an insect. "Pardon us," she said in a strained whisper, still bowing, and then shot her head straight up into the air, rolled back, and screamed. Howled. First a sharp yap then a throaty baying that wouldn't stop. For such a small person her lungs could evidently hold an amazing amount of air. Still on her knees, she arched backwards, bending over in a kind of reverse bow, until her head was nearly touching the floor mat, only on the wrong side. The screaming did not let up.

All the women closed their mouths and covered their noses and ran out.

Shimamura had jumped to his feet. He stood there. And watched. With her backwards half somersault, Kiyo had exposed most of her upper body, and he could not help looking at the white skin stretched over her ribs, and at two tiny dark nipples that seemed to have slipped alarmingly close to her neck. Her whole body seemed to have slipped out of joint. Her shoulders and elbows had shifted into places that human anatomy could not foresee. And where were her hands? Were they clenched inside the hollows of her knees? Bent backwards at the knuckles? Was she now going to turn herself inside out, like a glove? Shimamura did not try to help her. Her face flushed a deep red, her neck was distended, and as she rolled over sideways, still screaming, her sash started coming unwound. Under her kimono—a beautiful, pale-colored girl's kimono adorned with an appropriate fish pattern—he noticed several tightly wound bandages. The household probably expected her to lose her dress in the course of the day, and therefore made sure her underparts were well wrapped every morning.

The throaty yapping tipped back into a shrill yip, then began to quiver and finally faded off in a deep wheeze. Kiyo stretched out her neck. Her eyes rolled back. For a hopeful moment Shimamura had the impression a classic tonic seizure was about to occur as part of a normal epileptic contortion, but instead Kiyo lay down on her side, pulled her feet neatly under the hem of her kimono, propped her cheek on her hand and looked Shimamura straight in the face, exhausted and a little reproachful, as if all this debilitating commotion were his fault.

Dr. Shimamura heard himself exclaiming "Please come help your daughter." But the words came out small and hoarse, and no one came.

"Go on," said Kiyo mildly, "have a look."

She rolled over on her back and took off more clothing. She went so far as to gather the bandages together a bit, just below her hips, to the beginning of her pubic hair, and pulled the fish pattern wide apart, exposing her thighs.

And there came the fox.

While at rest the animal evidently resided right below Kiyo's underwraps—at least that was where he seemed to be working his way out. It was a small fox, two or three hand lengths, depending on whether he was stretched out or balled up, and in his cramped quarters just under Kiyo's tender white skin he moved a bit like a caterpillar. Kiyo traced his movements with her finger: across her stomach slowly up into her chest, into her right armpit and then the left and then with a jerk into her left upper arm, where the creature pushed nearly all the way to her elbow, until this swelled and swelled to the point of bursting. Shimamura thought he heard teeth gnashing. He stood stone still. Kiyo panted. She seemed to be in great pain, her forehead broke out in a sweat and her eyes filled with tears, but she did not utter another cry. And all the time her reproachful look: I'm putting up with all of this for you, Sensei, just for you.

Shun'ichi Shimamura kept one eye on himself as he witnessed the outline of a perfectly formed small fox appear, slanted, just below Kiyo's collarbone. After a short rest the fox dodged to the side, then climbed into her neck and tried to force his way into her mouth. Kiyo pressed her lips together, then pressed her hands to her mouth to contain the fox. Her cheeks swelled up, and a few tiny bubbles of pink foam oozed out between her fingers. Was it the fox's muzzle knocking against her teeth? Or had it turned around and was now pressing its strong tail against her lips? Kiyo was choking. Her body was shaking and twitching. Shimamura realized he had been muttering to himself the whole time—he hoped he hadn't been saying a prayer. Then the thing turned around and moved away from the mouth, down the throat, across the chest, and back into its lair under the white bandages. Kiyo stretched out and gave a gentle moan. Perhaps like a bear. Or a bear sow. A deeply satisfied moan or drone that sounded far too low to be her own came out of the girl's bloody lips:

"*Paroxysm*," said the fox.

The voice was gnarled, wise, ancient. He lay there in the form of a girl, all four legs stretched out, surrounded by the pale fish-patterned cloth and the tattered pages of a French magazine. Shun'ichi Shimamura peered into the elliptically shaped pupils encased in the dark, amber-colored eyes and met a gaze that was half interested, half bored.

Shimamura spent the better part of two and a half weeks in that bright room—or at least so his brain reconstructed. He sat beside the women, kneeling in his stocking feet, sweating and fanning himself, waiting to be granted an audience. When the women covered their noses and mouths with their kerchiefs and ran outside as if on command—because as much as they may have loved the girl, they had no desire to take over her fox—Shimamura would stand up and move closer to the mats in the middle of the room, near to Kiyo's little table.

New clothes had been found for the student, who now assisted occasionally—or often—or always, depending on what Shimamura remembered. Which meant that the youth also stood by and watched. Because watching was all Shimamura did. Only one version of his memory, and not a very reliable one at that, showed him descending on the girl with percussion hammer and specula, when she once lost consciousness and was reliably human, so that he could examine her eagerly, excitedly, but without success.

The student took photographs. They happily put up with that—they being Kiyo and her illness, which to the shame of all Japan was still known as fox possession, although it was surely hiding somewhere in Professor Griesinger's manual, even if Shimamura couldn't find it, since he was evidently not a good enough doctor and was perhaps suffering from heat stroke or possibly some folie à deux.

The student must have shot one roll of film after the other using Professor Sakaki's very modern English camera. Shimamura didn't remember anything else about him, no superstitious acts, no fraternizing with the patient, not even Kiyo crying on his chest. Kiyo's mania, her sheer existence had in one swoop turned the student from a fox exorcist back into the boy from Tokyo who for inexplicable reasons was following around a doctor of neurology.

The bright room, the fish-pattern garment, the marvel of Kiyo's anatomy: a photographic godsend. And on top of that she made conversation. Polite speech: about the weather, the flowers, the songbirds in the garden—what a consolation for the spirit—and the market risk of flatfish, horse mackerel, and monkfish. The girl's bright young voice and Shimamura's "indeed?"—and meanwhile the fox had carefully twisted Kiyo's hands into an obscene gesture she could not undo, so that Shimamura could not possibly forget its presence despite all the polite chitchat.

Now and then the fox called him "little uncle." More often, though, it was "my dear colleague." Even the occasional sexual proposition—like from some old whorish fox-woman. Then Kiyo would lower her head and excuse herself and clap her small white hands in front of her mouth to muffle her giggling, this bright, dumb little girl's giggle.

Shimamura pestered Kiyo's mother and aunts and servants as to why they didn't arrange for an exorcist. He combed the garden between Kiyo's favorite little flowers and songbirds, scouting for anything that might help—priests, magic pennants, receptacles. That was something he remembered exactly, running up to the steep bank by himself to look for receptacles. And that he would have gladly used his own bare hands to stuff tofu into the toothless maw of a desperate, leprous receptacle, just so that the damned fox would take a bite. And almost certainly shouting all alone into the quiet sunlight, between the dragonflies and the plucked fur in the branches: *A receptacle! Please! Over here! I need you!*

"She isn't getting exorcized because there's nothing to exorcize," said the student, poking around in his pipe. "There isn't any fox raging inside the girl. There's nothing to drive out. A fox doesn't live inside a fox. The fox is the girl's soul.

Better to leave it inside. Oh, Sensei, you've got it all wrong! In my family, four hundred years ago, people used to know about these things."

Shimamura was certain his memories of these speeches were all wrong. In which case was it really true that Kiyo had been allowed to play with the student in the garden, when she was doing better, with tops and shuttlecocks, and that they laughed and laughed?

On the next to last evening in the fishmonger's house a storm approached but did not erupt.

"What a shame," said Kiyo. "It would have cooled things down. Are you going back home to Tokyo soon, Sensei? Will you write me letters? Will you send me my photographs? Will you send me a new French magazine? The last one is so horribly chewed up …"

Shimamura remembered everyone eating together in the evening, the student, the women, Kiyo and himself, at a spot on the veranda where there was a little more air. And that the sky was electric, black and electric, and someone—the student, one of the women, Shimamura—remarked "Ideal weather for ball lightning."

Dr. Shimamura hadn't slept for two weeks, and that night was no exception. He lay down, sat up, lay back down, sat on the porch and fanned himself. There was no ball lightning. The moon was nearly full, clouds went drifting by, and Shimamura gazed up at the roof with the fish ornament standing on its head. Every night he looked at the fish. Its mouth was open, its tailfin spread wide, and against the moonlight it looked like a crooked fountain.

Then he saw the girl crossing the roof on all fours, silently creeping along the ridge, hand over hand, toe over toe. In the middle of the roof, where the eaves widened, she stopped. And groomed herself, first licking her little paws before using them to wipe her face. The moon came and went, the broad fishtail and the girl both silhouetted against the light. Then she took off her clothes. She removed her nightgown, the bedsheet, whatever it was she wore when she went out on the roof at night. She took off her human skin as well, through a smooth opening on her stomach, and shook off her human hair, and after she had freed herself she groomed her ears. A whorl of fur above the collarbone. Around the jaws and down the sternum the color went from gold to white, and a *linea alba* ran down the entire golden tail all the way to the tip. Then Shimamura saw someone approach her. Someone who had been hanging on the eaves and now with painstaking effort scaled the ridge, a clumsy person who couldn't control his hands and feet and who slipped when he tried to nuzzle her, then went rolling over the shingles like a wet sack.

Who was it? The student? Shimamura himself? An animal?

For a while she let the person dangle there. She laughed and barked. Then she helped him up. And the moon hid behind a cloud.

The next morning Shun'ichi Shimamura woke up with a pharyngeal spasm and discovered that the student had disappeared. The spasm was quickly remedied with a cup of water; the student did not resurface. At first they thought he'd gone to the cliffs to enjoy the view or that he'd set off to Saiwa, but when the camera was found half disassembled in the anteroom of the kitchen, people began to wonder. The entire household knew how much the student loved his camera, why would he leave without taking it?

Shun'ichi Shimamura couldn't remember what efforts he made to track down the student. He only remembered the fever that set off the spasm and how the women were suddenly clinging to him like leeches, with complaints, requests, questions, confessions and offers.

"And that's how it's been ever since," Shimamura said to the housemaid when she once again brought the morning water bucket and furtively stared at the bedridden retiree, as though he were the most beautiful thing in the world. "That's how it's been, Luise, to this very day. My fever. My allure for women. And the student was never seen again."

After he'd decided for better or worse to return home by himself, Shimamura paid Kiyo one last visit. She had been moved from the bright room into a dark chamber, because she couldn't stand the light. He found her emaciated, apathetic, with poor circulation and unclean skin. He tapped the facial nerve in front of the ear lobe. Kiyo cried. She, too, clung somewhat to Shimamura, but soon let him go. She whined after her stuffed monkey. She whined after tofu. Nothing satisfied her. Then she fell asleep. Shimamura told the women to mix egg and honey and feed it to the girl. Now her fox was gone as well.

In the rickshaw, halfway to Tokyo, he wrote his last diagnosis for Professor Sakaki: hysteria.

5

For years Hanako Shimamura had been working on a biography of her son. She had been working on it for so many years that she was long past the point where everything seemed to spread out too far in length and breadth, and was gradually coming to the opinion that the entire enterprise was more worthy of thirty pages than three hundred, and that it had been overrated from the beginning.

Of course Hanako wrote in secret. If she was pleased with a particular passage she would hide it in Shun'ichi's cast-off plant press, which was wrapped in a bolt of green fabric and stashed beneath the floor in the north room. Passages that failed to meet her approval—which meant most of them— she tossed into the fire.

At first she had planned a kind of festschrift on the occasion of Shun'ichi's retirement. Perhaps they could have secretly let her coach one of the speakers, so that he would give a decent speech instead of jabbering on and on about the wall mats. But the festschrift degenerated into a kind of bildungsroman, which in turn evolved into a family saga. And that got bogged down in a pile of lies. And suddenly what Hanako had were her own memoirs, in which her only son Shun'ichi was a marginal figure, even though he was clearly in the center of her life. Here and there she came up with sentences that might easily be mistaken for poetry and which reduced life in general and Shun'ichi's life in particular to declarations in which the word "not" made a frequent appearance.

Year after year Hanako Shimamura looked on as her son continued with his life and her hand continued with her writing. Because Shun'ichi didn't speak with her—not in Tokyo, not in Kyoto, and not even in Kameoka—after all, what was he supposed to speak with her about, what was there to discuss with one's mother?—Hanako had to speculate on both his life and its meaning.

A life, she ascertained, particularly that of an educated man and especially that of her son, should follow a simple motto. And this motto, she determined after lengthy consideration and very many novels, ought to have some element of nobility and some element of desperation. Because nobility without desperation was uninteresting; it grew dusty and lost its allure.

For nearly eight years Hanako Shimamura brooded over an appropriate motto for Shun'ichi's life that would guide her brush and prevent so many pages from landing in the kitchen stove.

For a long time she clung to *Obligation and Inclination*. That practically presented itself. Nearly everything was a matter of *Obligation and Inclination*, so why not Shun'ichi's life? Unfortunately Hanako couldn't find a single incidence of *Inclination* in this particular life. Even things Shun'ichi appeared inclined toward always came out of obligation. "Isn't that the case?" she muttered, while her voice grew more and more shaky and her hand more and more gnarled, and her head sank onto the manuscript. Desperation, for certain. And nobility, too, of course: for example the beautiful wall mats in Kyoto that protected raving patients from hurting themselves. But she didn't find any conflict between obligation and inclination, and without conflict a motto was worthless. For some time—three or four years—she thought of inclinations she might ascribe to her son—bad, irresponsible passions that contradicted all sense of duty, which took all his strength to keep in check, which explained why he succumbed to fever and was not as scientifically active as his colleagues—but Hanako didn't understand anything about such things and she hoped Shun'ichi didn't either. And so one day she decided to discard that motto.

Then she came up with *Genius and Insanity*.

At the end of February 1922, when the weather suddenly turned very beautiful, Hanako Shimamura sat every night beside her daughter-in-law's mother Yukiko and, following this new maxim, cheerily penned her thoughts. Hanako wrote:

After Dr. Shimamura had cured thirty-three patients in the Shimane Prefecture, all of whom believed they were possessed by the fox-demon, he returned to Tokyo a broken man. The reason for this was as follows: the young medical student Yoshiro Takaoka, who had accompanied him, had disappeared, (quite possibly by falling to his death from a high place, but his body was never recovered). Although Professor Hajime Sakaki, Dean of Neurology at the Imperial University in Tokyo and Dr. Shimamura's honorable teacher, absolved him of any guilt and also took on the painful correspondence with the Takaoka family, a mania formed in Dr. Shimamura's consciousness that he alone was responsible for the disappearance or death of the student. To wit: Dr. Shimamura's constitution, which for some time had teetered precariously between genius and madness, had, during the course of treating all the patients, and especially the last one—a very difficult case—gradually tilted more and more toward madness, until he finally . . .

Hanako scratched out *genius* and replaced it with *genial talent*. After all she was describing her own son, so she oughtn't to brag that way.

. . . until even he was no longer able to distance himself from the so-called fox, and consequently developed the IDÉE FIXE *that he had personally swallowed every patient's fox following each extraction, only to carry them home to Tokyo and bear them for the rest of his life at the cost of his mental and physical health. He believed that the disappearance of the student Takaoka was connected with the foxes, which absolutely no one could understand. In a feverish state he howled away at us for nights on end, spouting the same nonsense, and we were all very glad that the honorable Professor Sakaki never found out about it, because otherwise Dr. Shimamura's career would have ended then and there.*

Hanako crossed out the last sentence. Then she took out "genial talent" and once again replaced it with "genius," to better balance the matter, and tried a few other expressions for IDÉE FIXE.

The fact was that Dr. Shimamura had not only brought us a form of madness from Shimane, but also something that could be called soft and beautiful. This was in truth very new for him. (Cf. chapter "Dr. Shimamura's Childhood: a rawboned boy of rigid temperament.") And it was this new, soft, and beautiful quality that he carried with him ever after. And even though his life came to naught, with no natural or scientific heirs, it was always infused with this beautiful, soft, sympathetic and almost feminine madness, which somewhat ...

Yukiko wheezed and stopped breathing for a moment. Then she began to snore. Hanako sighed and pulled the blanket off Yukiko's face so she wouldn't suffocate. Hanako always sat next to Yukiko's futon whenever she wrote. She liked to keep an eye on Yukiko when she was sleeping, since after all most old people wound up dying in their sleep. Unlike Hanako, who preferred to brood over things, Yukiko liked to sleep. Every evening she warmed up her sake and swallowed her veronal. That's why she never woke up, while Hanako sat close to her head, writing and keeping an eye on her.

... which somewhat inhibited his genius but did his female patients much good, Hanako finished the sentence.

"Damnation," she whispered, when she suddenly realized that *Genius and Insanity* was also devoid of any conflict.

Yukiko gasped. Then she stopped breathing again. Hanako waited a moment before giving her a light slap. She heard Shun'ichi's clock strike four times in the walled-in room where he lived and contemplated.

"*Ach*, Shun'ichi," Hanako whispered.

She set her brush in the little jade basin decorated with mallow leaves and a frog. Why did she always write? She looked at the ink bleeding into the water and wiped the bristles against the frog's head. Because he deserves it, thought

Hanako. Because he's my son. Because everyone deserves it. Every life. "Exactly," said Hanako. Yukiko made a rattling sound, first with her nose, then in her throat, then she passed gas under the blanket.

Even Yukiko was deserving of a life history, thought Hanako. Even Sei, the little nurse from Kyoto everyone thought was a patient because her face looked a little imbecilic and her legs were crooked and her breasts so large. In fact Sei deserved an entire novel, Hanako thought all of a sudden—one containing love, misery, silence, and suicide. Every morning Sei tried to flatten her breasts beneath her *sarashi*, but they always popped out. That's why Shun'ichi called her Anna or Luise. With breasts so utterly foreign, Sei didn't have a chance. Perhaps *East and West* would make a good motto? Hanako Shimamura decided to give it a try, perhaps even tomorrow night. She gathered the pages she had written—in any case there were only five—and stacked them neatly before tossing them into the fire.

6

With instances of induced insanity (folie communiquée, folie à deux), according to Dr. Griesinger, *the secondary cases are in the rule slow-witted people with very limited powers of psychic resistance, chiefly women.*

Shimamura was in the port of Alexandria sitting in a kind of roadside tea house that reminded him of a capsized sailboat, attempting to drink a cup of coffee. On his first try he wound up with nothing but the grounds in his mouth, which he spat out a little less inconspicuously than he would have wished. Then he stirred and waited. Once again he picked up the cup and peered inside. A metal demitasse with a metal handle. Shimamura dabbed his spoon in the coffee, then lifted a bit of the liquid from the top and held it in the beam of sunlight coming from between two sails of a boat. The coffee was pale and he could see the grounds floating inside. He sank his spoon into the cup and stirred once more, halfway up so as not to muddle the bottom. Then he lit a cigarette and went on waiting.

The Imperial Commission had granted him a stipend and now, four months after his return from Shimane, he was finally en route to Paris.

In people with such weak dispositions, Dr. Griesinger continued, *there is seldom any further autonomous processing of the delusional ideas. On the contrary, when such individuals are removed from the influence of the primary cases, they are generally soon back on the rails.*

Shimamura was unfamiliar with the phrase "back on the rails." He pictured Dr. Griesinger, whose lithographic portrait adorned the frontispiece—a soft-eyed, baldish man with fluffy sideburns—riding in old trains on old tracks through the German Empire, intent on projecting great strength of character. And yet his beard hid a weak chin and his neck was certainly too long and his larynx too pointed, no matter how stiffly he strangled himself with his collars.

Do you also remember, Sensei, when you were little, the screwneck ghost? The one that creeps up from behind and suddenly grabs you by the throat and then stares you right in the eye? Do you remember? Do you?

"No," said Shun'ichi Shimamura. He stuffed the Griesinger in his briefcase and the student in the bottommost compartment of his brain. Carefully he again picked up the little cup and slurped the cooling coffee, swallowing a lot of air as he did so, taking pains not to tilt the demitasse too much—that proved effective. Perhaps this was the moment when he forgot the name of the student, beyond all recall.

During four months of tediously concealed insanity in Kyoto, he had managed to accept his constitutional weakness. Dr. Griesinger's portrait, as embarrassing as this was, had been of great help. Even weak-chinned, long-necked, suggestible neurologists could do a lot of good, Dr. Shimamura sermonized to himself for four months, as he put off seeing his patients—especially the female ones—with a thousand excuses, while cobbling together articles based on earlier research findings so that Professor Sakaki and the commission wouldn't notice he had contracted something dreadful in Shimane.

So, now let Europe infect me, he thought, with all its European correctness. He lit another cigarette and leafed through the French dictionary he had acquired earlier, along with the good cigarettes, a fez, and postcards of the pyramids.

For days he had been waiting for the passage to Genoa. He had found lodgings in a guest house located in a loud neighborhood far from the harbor, just because some child who was evidently responsible for such matters had led him there, with lots of shouting. The guest house was infested with fleas. Shimamura was happy that he wasn't as concerned with hygiene as so many of his colleagues, that he didn't have to worry about foreign fleas, and that he didn't have to bother Robert Koch in Berlin. Viewed from Tokyo it appeared that entire swarms of young Japanese hygienists were buzzing around Professor Koch, in the hope he might teach them something about bacteria. Shimamura was grateful that among all those who had received a stipend, he was the only one in his particular field, and therefore had no need of joining any swarm.

These days Shun'ichi Shimamura was frequently happy or thankful. If he had permitted himself, he would have wept tears of joy or thankfulness or even from being suddenly moved by small, everyday things, like puddles or fallen leaves.

He felt like an old man with arteriosclerosis or a woman in menopause. And just as he carried his fever, which never dipped below 100°, he would also carry this particular flaw wherever he went—to Genoa and on to France and then to Germany.

Strictly speaking, Dr. Shimamura was the only neurologist in Japan. Professor Sakaki did place a great value on a multidisciplinary mastery of all subjects, especially gynecology. And he had studied with Robert Koch and visited all the other important places abroad very long ago. Professor Sakaki had been the first to experience and master everything. He could also afford to insert some Japanese folklore into the field of neurology, so unshakable was his disposition. "Here, Shimamura," Sakaki had said, "is a nice English portfolio you can put a few woodcuts in. Buy a few dirty prints when you're in Nagasaki. You're a medical man, after all. And see that you get some with a bit of foxy hanky-panky—that's bound to be a hit. Play the oriental when you're in Europe. Then all your colleagues will be at your feet, and the women as well, especially the women." After that Sakaki had laughed hard and Shimamura had laughed along; after all, Professor Sakaki was his teacher.

Now laughter came to him nearly as easily as crying. His elevated temperature was accompanied by a constant throbbing in his neck, a constriction, as if some alien giggling were trying to free itself; this complaint was lessened by genuine laughter. So he was grateful whenever Professor Sakaki actually gave him cause to laugh, with advice that proved funny or that dealt with women. And he laughed when Sakaki forced him to write a study on "the influence of repression of the sexual drive on the nerves and psyche"—first when he started collecting data and then when nothing came of it.

Shimamura stubbed out his third cigarette, then left the sailboat-teahouse and walked over to the information booth. "Genoa, Genoa" he begged, and was given an answer he did not understand. Then he went to the checkroom to look after his bags. But he didn't go inside. Instead Shun'ichi Shimamura stood in the sunlight in front of the shack where his two trunks were probably stored, staring out in silence. In his trunks were an English portfolio with fifteen utterly filthy woodcuts, a bundle with a chewed-up toy, and a photograph of a fish ornament on the ridge of a roof. The ridge was long, straight and generally uninteresting. All the other photos from Shimane had come out black. Evidently the student had no idea how to operate Professor Sakaki's wonderful English camera.

Dr. Shimamura stood quietly in front of the port of Alexandria's transcontinental luggage checkroom, imagining his luggage. For a moment he wondered whether he couldn't simply stay where he was and imagine Europe—Paris and Berlin, Heidelberg, Munich, and Vienna, with their respective universities and insane asylums—without actually travelling there, and then whether he might imagine the rest of his life without actually living it. A laugh or a cry rose in his throat and sank on command back into his chest. He set off for his lodgings. At least ten screaming boys who earned their pittance here knew all about the Japanese man and Genoa. When the ship arrived they would come for him. They would come fetch him with a lot of clamor and commotion and escort him through the streets the same way. Shimamura felt he could rely on that.

He found his lodgings, took his temperature, put on his fez and smoked and brooded. Then a boy showed up shouting that the ship to Genoa was already there.

By the time he left the Suez canal, which had confounded his sense of geography, Shimamura had already given up counting the days. From early to late, under an eternally blue sky, over an eternally blue sea in which nothing seemed to live—no fish, no whales, not even seaweed or algae—he once again took pains to distract himself, from himself, from his actual life, even as it was taking place, without taking much notice of it or of his tribulations ... and now this entire life was being transported around the globe, courtesy of the Imperial House. Shimamura took pains to avoid thinking about that as well.

The Egyptian cigarettes had all been smoked. The two Japanese novels that the unfriendly stranger he was married to had given him to take on the journey—without so much as a smile—had been read, forgotten, and lost, and were now likely jammed behind the bunk of a middle class cabin floating back and forth on the Suez canal. The days were too warm, the nights too cold. The starry sky also demanded so much attention he had no desire to venture on deck at night. There was too much eating. Now and then the orchestra would play. Both the food and the music gave him the shudders, but Shimamura tried to come to terms with that, since it was undoubtedly a question of acclimatization. Soon however the shudders gave way to a great indifference, which he could not overcome despite the best will in the world.

There was a German on board who did business in Egypt. Shimamura conversed with the man day in and day out, as it was impossible to talk with anyone else. The German complimented Shimamura so profusely on his command of the language that Shimamura began to suspect his German was less good than he had thought. The German was no longer young; the right half of his face seemed somewhat rigid and drooping. In addition, his left hand had a light tremor. Taken together it made little sense. Shimamura began to avoid him, and then suddenly the German started avoiding Shimamura, as if he had only waited to avoid him until he himself was avoided, so as not to be impolite. Shimamura discovered a budding sympathy for Viennese waltzes in his heart. He now spent much time with the orchestra, fighting urges to laugh or cry or sway in time to the music. Then came Italy, Genoa, and the train.

By an accident that bordered on a miracle, immediately upon his arrival in Paris he found the two Tokyo law students whom he had telegraphed about his coming. The two Japanese faces were staring directly into the window of his compartment. Shimamura simply had to step out of the train to greet his compatriots.

The Gare du Nord was large, the buildings were large, the city was large, and everything was made of stone and looked Christian — nothing but churches that screamed to high heaven. That's more or less what Shimamura's brain rambled on about while he sat in the carriage with the two law students. "The buildings strike you as large and everything looks like it's made of stone, doesn't it?" said one. The students were young men who probably hadn't been living there long either, and they were all aflutter to have a newcomer under their wing. Shimamura found out that he would be sharing lodgings with them. He couldn't remember who had arranged that, but he pretended not to be taken aback. Nor did he let himself be taken aback by the large buildings. Finally he said "Oh, oh" just to be polite.

Inside the apartment near the Sorbonne that Shimamura was destined to share with the law students, and specifically inside the room where he was supposed to sleep, there was a bidet. It was a porcelain basin mounted inside a chair and covered with a lid, in which one washed one's bottom. The bidet was near and dear to the law students, who showed it to Shimamura before he even had a chance to take off his coat. Whoever wanted to wash his bottom at night, they said, would have to do so in Shimamura's bedroom. Then they laughed so hard they cried. They were silly boys. Perhaps the utter ridiculousness of this French creation, with its turned legs and daintily tapered basin, boosted their Japanese pride. Or maybe they were drunk. Shimamura laughed along for a moment, then praised the hygiene of the fixture. He thought it might come in useful to position himself right away as a wet blanket. Afterward he excused himself, as he wanted to unpack and rest up a bit. Nor did he let himself be lured out of his room later on, when the law students wanted to go to a nightclub called the Cabaret of Hell, which was decorated with stone and papier-mâché devils hung from the ceiling, among other things. Shimamura stayed behind, sitting at his window, eating Genoa cheese, and staring at the bidet, not without emotion.

§

"Reaction times, Luise," Shimamura said to the water bucket, which he had grown used to looking at instead of the maid-servant, when she entered the room. "Reaction times, guinea pigs, and chess. For a very long time that was the only research I was pursuing in Paris, and I was convinced that Japan had no need of it and that my stipend was an utter waste."

She tied her sleeves back with a narrow sash and began stirring the water with both hands. Lately she had been doing that every morning. Shimamura suspected that she did it to show him that the water was pleasant and not too hot and good to use for whatever purpose he wished.

"Reaction times, Luise," said Shimamura, "are data collected for use in psychometrics, chess is a game like shogi, and guinea pigs are mindless, tailless rats."

Luise shuddered. Perhaps she was horrified. Perhaps the water was ice cold. Perhaps she didn't understand. Perhaps she had long ago contracted consumption.

"But then again it isn't all that bad," said Shimamura.

7

Dr. Shimamura had lost no time finding his countrymen at the Gare du Nord; what he didn't find in Paris even after days and weeks was neurology.

After an astoundingly long sleep, he woke up feeling somewhat cheery, and the first thing he did was walk to the Sorbonne as Professor Sakaki had instructed. In his briefcase he was carrying two letters to the medical faculty, and safely tucked under his arm—because they didn't quite fit in the briefcase—the collection of dirty woodcuts from Nagasaki, as a possible last resort for winning over his French colleagues.

The Sorbonne looked like a church and seemed a great waste of stone, but by now that barely elicited a smile from Shimamura. The French language was another matter. It bothered him. In fact it bothered him more and more and ultimately proved to be an insurmountable barrier. The letters of recommendation were in German, Shimamura spoke German, and no one at the Sorbonne understood that language. And when he finally located the Faculty of Medicine—after much traipsing around during which he was observed by many people old and young and undoubtedly also thoroughly discussed—it turned out that even there no one understood a word of German. As a result on his very first day—and many subsequent ones—he had to resort to broken Latin, which went so badly on all sides that Shimamura was on the verge of tossing his fox pornography on the table and shouting for help in Japanese. Instead he bowed politely and left.

He bought some cigarettes, a city map called *Paris Monumental*, and some bread and cheese. The bread and cheese did him good; it purified his spirit like some cleansing self-mortification. He headed to the Jardin du Luxembourg, smoked, ate, and pondered. He couldn't recall whether the misconception that German was the worldwide lingua franca of neurology came from his own imagining or from Professor Sakaki. Shimamura observed the thickly beveled basin of the fountain and wondered how hygienic all this stone might be, and whether the quarries that presumably riddled the French countryside were secure, profitable, and strategically planned, or if instead they represented anarchy and the beginning of the end. Someone said "*chinois*" to him and Shimamura answered "*merci*" because he didn't know anything better. Then he went home and engaged Sato, the younger of the two jurists, as an interpreter.

Even with Sato's help Dr. Shimamura couldn't find anything that resembled neurology. He did find a lecture, which judging from the various brains on display at the front of the hall was designed for neophytes, and he also found a convivial group of professors who wanted to talk about Japanese theater, which they knew from the Exposition Universelle.

Noticing that Shimamura was growing increasingly mistrustful of his French, Sato started sniggering at Shimamura's inept planning and his lack of language and about neurology in general. Why does Japan need all this neurology, Sato asked in a roundabout manner, and Shimamura answered in an equally roundabout manner that French jurisprudence would surely provide the answer. After that Shimamura and Sato no longer got along and had an unfriendly parting of ways.

Then Dr. Shimamura discovered a neuropathological laboratory. There they were decapitating dogs. Then they decapitated chickens. Finally someone brought a sack of guinea pigs—this is where Shimamura first met that animal—and cut off the heads of those, too. Three dainty guillotines, true mechanical wonders, stood on three pedestals and dispatched the heads, leaving the bodies to become the focus of analysis; the heart and the vagus nerve were of special interest. The laboratory was not in good condition, it smelled bad and the overall atmosphere—attracting more visitors than scientists—was generally unsettling. There were even women among the guests, and men who seemed dressed from another era, probably poets, thought Shimamura. He couldn't understand why they would choose to dawdle about here, together with their concubines, in this awful room. He beheaded a guinea pig and checked the reflexes of head and body, which wasn't easy with the small furred animal. He also couldn't understand why they let him do this, why no one noticed that some completely unknown Oriental was playing with a guillotine. Once more someone called out "chinois!" but it didn't sound like a reproach. Shimamura replied "*excusez-moi.*" Then he added "*folie.*" How quickly could he learn this language, and was it even worth the effort? On the wall, just above the dog-sized guillotine, was a photograph in a cloth frame showing a bearded melancholic; the picture was adorned with black ribbon. Probably the founding father of this enterprise. The walls were spattered with blood. This day, too, ended in the Jardin du Luxembourg, with meditation and cheese.

Dr. Shimamura refused to give up on the Sorbonne. Far away from the department of decapitation, in a completely separate building, he discovered a facility still under construction that didn't appear to belong to any particular faculty but was evidently assigned to physiological psychology. This subject felt new, having just been invented the previous year in Germany, which is why the two researchers in charge spoke a little bit of German. When Shimamura appeared out of nowhere—he had left both the recommendation letters and the woodcuts at home, so the only strategy left was to simply show up—he was well received. Apparently the physiological psychologists had no staff apart from a single lab technician who would occasionally sidle in and then disappear for long periods. So the researchers took what they could get, even if that meant a Japanese neurologist.

Each of the physiological psychologists—Shimamura repeated this tongue-twister over and over until it rolled elegantly off his lips—sported a beard and a pince-nez, and each seemed self-assured despite their empty, sad, partially unplastered rooms. Their names were Dr. Beaunis and Dr. Bidet, which Shimamura took in with an iron countenance. Then he locked himself in the toilet and burst into laughter that verged on the hysterical. And then he was moved to feel compassion and respect for this man fated to spend a lifetime in France with such a surname. Perhaps the name was not uncommon. Perhaps it even came from an old medical family, one of whose scions had devoted himself to rectal hygiene and now another to physiological psychology. For an excessively long period, constantly in danger of breaking into burbling, tear-inducing laughter, Dr. Shimamura thought about Dr. Bidet's name while at the same time attempting to make himself useful in the laboratory.

The work consisted of measuring reaction times, which, as the name suggested, was the time it took for someone to react to something. To keep refining the measuring technique and the evaluation of the data, both stimulus and reaction were kept simple: the stimulus was for instance a little ball, which upon command was dropped into a pipe, and the reaction was pushing a button. The laboratory housed a host of small machines generating stimuli and collecting reactions. Some looked like telegraphs, others like gramophones, a few like small pianos. The ones that spit out the little balls looked like guillotines; Shimamura almost had to return to the toilet for another good laugh.

Doctors Beaunis and Bidet recorded Shun'ichi Shimamura's reaction times fifty times each on ten separate devices. They gave him his own sheet of data, to which a little box had been added noting his Japanese origin. According to Dr. Beaunis, until at least twenty more Japanese (or at least Asians) were tested, Shimamura's reaction times would be completely unusable, unless they simply erased the little box with "Japanese." After thus giving Shimamura a guilty conscience, Dr. Beaunis induced him to recruit other test subjects, so that he might at least contribute something to the success of the project as a whole, and without any fuss sent him to canvass the halls of the Sorbonne. "Anyone will do," said Dr. Beaunis, and Bidet agreed. They wrote out a sentence in French for their guest, which he could to use to entice the others, and left him to his fate.

And so Shun'ichi Shimamura spent three days roaming through the Sorbonne and recruiting on behalf of the physiological psychologists. He had remarkable success. Everyone he approached chose to come. They clustered after him—students, teachers, staff. In fact so many people crowded all at once into the laboratory of Dr. Beaunis and Dr. Bidet to have their reaction times measured that the fall tachistoscope lost its calibration and the kymograph lost one of its legs. Test subjects had to be trained as measuring assistants or else the onslaught could never have been managed. Thanks to Shimamura more data was collected in three days than had been in an entire year—whenever he went walking down the corridor armed with his French sentence, people were lurking in wait, ready to pounce. Beaunis and Bidet invited him to dine in an elegant establishment. The next morning he woke up feeling insulted. He felt like a market crier. He doubted the relevance of reaction times. What was a neurologist, what was Japan supposed to do with healthy people watching little falling balls? Then it turned out that Dr. Bidet's name was actually Binet. Perhaps his pince-nez was overly tight and constricted his nose when he spoke. But it was mostly this mishearing, which in the toilet of the Sorbonne had practically unleashed his inner beast, that caused Shun'ichi Shimamura to feel so out of sorts that he drew up a formal letter of resignation, which he had Sato translate into French and drop off at the laboratory for physiological psychology. The Imperial commission, he said in a roundabout manner, is indisposed to fund such a discipline.

From that point on Dr. Shimamura attended medical lectures. He didn't understand them, and moreover he already knew the material: after all he was no longer a student. He drafted a general memorandum on the organization of medical study at the Sorbonne, which drifted somewhat into philosophical rumination.

He chose not to spend his free time with the law students. They were acquainted with a number of other Japanese in Paris who were studying law, with whom they passed many long, drunken evenings, mostly in the Cabaret of Hell—in addition to an establishment that evidently provided soy sauce. In the new Japan, the legal profession was to be modeled after French jurisprudence, which is why the city was swarming with so many budding lawyers. They gawped at the girls, concocted theories about them, and spread gossip from Tokyo which they kept receiving by letter. One enjoyed reading poems out loud that he then sent to Tokyo—verses that used elevated language to extol events there, for instance the birth of his dissertation advisor's son and heir. Shimamura concluded that their company was also not part of his charge from the Imperial commission.

He sat in the Jardin du Luxembourg, eating his bread and cheese while yearning for tofu—all the more so after hearing the words *soy sauce*—and studied the German articles on memory strategies of blindfold chess players that Beaunis and his colleague had given him. The texts were based on correspondence between famous blindfold chess players and psychologists, as well as on laboratory experiments in which chess masters who were frequently engrossed in many games at once gave a running account as to how they stored the past moves inside their brains. The articles were difficult to decipher, which made the results seem more important. To Shimamura, who didn't know how to play chess, they were hardly comprehensible. The blindfold chess players summoned pictures of chessboards they had never seen in real life, gleefully augmenting their games with phrases such as "bishop's gambit." With increasing anxiety, his tongue hallucinating about tofu, Shimamura studied these articles—forcing himself not to take them metaphorically, as a personal indictment, an insult to his own confused game. He stashed the bundle with Kiyo's playthings in his briefcase and carried it wherever he went.

Shimamura went for many walks along the grand boulevards. He didn't mind being seen holding his copy of *Paris Monumental* right in front of his nose. He traveled everywhere on foot. He went to the Eiffel Tower, crossed the Seine and systematically walked each ray emanating from the star of the Place de l'Étoile. On top of its magnificence, Paris was one grand cabinet of curiosities. Bit by bit he squandered a considerable amount of money to see everything he could, half out of interest, half out of a sense of duty, and occasionally as a self-punishment. He visited the wax museum, the Laterna Magica, the Diorama, the Panorama, the Kinetograph, and the morgue that housed the bodies recovered from the Seine. Then he went to a toy shop and bought toys—a locomotive, an astronomic gyroscope, alphabet dice in a little box, and a Noah's ark with a collection of loose animals. He stuffed everything into his briefcase. Then he drank some coffee and crème de menthe and went back to the Diorama, because his ticket was still valid. There he stood for a long time in front of a scene of carnage based on a work by Émile Zola, where intricate lighting revealed different layers painted on the semi-transparent canvas.

The boulevards were teeming with women and dogs. The women spoke loudly, revealing teeth as well as gums, wore dresses that were full in back, and paraded in large, military steps. Their dogs were tiny, fluffy, and mostly white. They were called *toutous*. The women dragged them by the leash, pressed them to their bosoms, held them in gloved hands, under their arms, clamped in the crook of their elbows, swaddled in shawls like babies. Some of the *toutous* wore jewelry, some were dressed in uniforms. And all of them—*toutous* and women alike—wanted to make Dr. Shimamura's acquaintance.

Apart from the small pink tongues of the *toutous* who licked him wherever they could manage, and which still haunted his dreams decades later, large stretches of this part of his stay in Paris remained foggy.

Shun'ichi Shimamura exuded a special magnetism that basically seemed to sweep aside the language barrier. *Chinois* and *merci* were all that were needed to set things in motion, and then there was no end to the reverberations. He had once had to accustom his mouth to German, and now Shimamura was also able to imitate French. He repeated words, adding *oui* or *non* at random, as he fended off the little dogs that were craning their necks to reach him or, when they were set down, trying to embrace his legs or attempting to mount his briefcase. Over and again time seemed to come to a standstill whenever a woman plunged into conversation with the Japanese doctor. In the Diorama, at the morgue, over crème de menthe and even on the other side of the Seine at the old fairgrounds where wild asses were on display, under streaming rain, united under a single umbrella, the world stopped for this or that Parisienne and the neurologist from the Far East. A conversation then ensued, so Shimamura understood, between something in him and something in her—a conversation that needed no French and no Japanese. And the *toutous*, when they escaped and climbed into his arms and licked him to their hearts' content, whispered things in his ears that someone inside understood. Shimamura's neck throbbed. His fever rose and fell, rose and fell, his memory frantically trying to reach back, so as not to have to take in the present: it recalled the word *receptacle*. Then it remembered the article about the consequences of sexual abstinence and clung to that for dear life.

Ultimately a heavyset, beautiful blonde with a lymphatic complexion took Shimamura along. Her *toutou*, a yellowish thing, ran ahead on a taut leash. Shimamura next found himself in a stone house, climbing a long, curved staircase, and then in a dark room full of ferns and fabric, a vast amount of warm fabric. He kept trying to figure out what the place was—a whorehouse, a rich family's living room, a theater dressing room, a furniture warehouse? Then he gave up. On one of the pieces of furniture, a long mahogany chair, he peeled the blonde out of her dress, undoing her bodice with his physician's fingers. "How could you …" said Shimamura's brain, taking its leave. There was a moment of impetuosity, some scuffling, drastic, not nice. Whatever it was struggled. Whatever it was conversed. There were tears. The blonde woman's skin was streaked with deep red wheals, as if she'd been swiped by a bear. "Dermographism," said Shimamura's brain, which had reappeared. And for a moment was ashamed. Then it disappeared again. And everything started all over. A stem on his glasses broke and this time when someone howled it was no longer clear who.

The *toutou* watched. It sat there quietly and watched, its forepaws neatly parallel, with its tiny, yellowed face.

When it was all over they rushed apart without saying a word.

That same evening, after he had taken his eyeglasses to an optician who repaired them on the spot, Shun'ichi Shimamura had the idea of taking the tram. He rode back across the Seine. Then he boarded a different car. Following in the wake of the women and dogs, subduing his hallucinations, Dr. Shimamura rode many different trams: St. Michel, Port Royal, St. Marcel. There he climbed out and found a splendid stone structure with a tall cupola. That was the Hôpital de la Salpêtrière, a women's asylum with five thousand beds. In Tokyo hardly a day had passed without Professor Sakaki mentioning its name.

8

"In our house," said Sachiko Shimamura, "everyone has gotten used to hiding things, mostly under the floor, and everyone knows where the things are hidden and fingers them in secret."

She was sitting on the west porch with her mother and stepmother. Because it was much too warm for the beginning of March they were imbibing soft drinks, one "strawberry" and two "original." Sachiko, Hanako and Yukiko had performed the requisite ceremony—pounding the stopper inside with their fist and freeing the glass marble which then danced with every swallow—and now they were drinking out of the bottle like young girls.

"Taking the trouble to hide things makes no sense," said Sachiko, "at least not for us, although with Shimamura the habit is probably already too engrained."

"These days I can't find anything as it is," said Yukiko.

They all laughed and drank. The three marbles clinked.

"What a beautiful summer sound,"

"Ah yes."

"Ah yes."

Outside by the clothes pole where she had hung out the bed linens, Sei was singing her song about Uji and Kei. Sachiko had forbidden her to sing, but had then changed her mind and encouraged her to sing whenever she wanted to. Sachiko Shimamura, the most patient person in the world, had recently become somewhat impatient and her moods were now a little fickle. Sei's sweet and slightly eerie voice wafted over as she sang the only song she knew.

"Hanako," said Sachiko, smiling, "you recently wrote in Shimamura's biography that the song about Uji and Kei was an important part of his childhood. Then Shimamura dug out your pages from under the floor of the north room, while you sat in the southern room reading your novel, and now he believes that 'Uji and Kei' were an important part of his childhood. But in reality there is no such song."

"That's too complicated for me," declared Yukiko. "May I please be excused?"

"How do you know what he believes?" asked Hanako.

"He's so reluctant to leave his own room that unless he was looking for some information he wouldn't keep digging out your pages from under that floor."

"May I please be excused?" Yukiko repeated stubbornly.

"Every winter you fix up the fox girl's toys that he hides behind the Charcot," said Hanako gently to Sachiko. "You've been doing it for years. You buy a new toy and carefully make it look broken and dirty and then you stick it in his bookcase in place of the old toy. That must put him on edge. He can hardly guess what's going on. What a strange experiment."

"Of course, Mother, you are excused," Sachiko said to Yukiko. "Go and have a nap."

Yukiko sighed. She let her marble clatter without drinking. Now she felt obliged to stay, even if that meant suffering for a few more hours; now she wouldn't dream of taking a nap.

"As long as he's on edge," said Sachiko, "he won't lose his will to live. You must know that better than anyone. You keep rewriting his biography just because you know he keeps reading it. No one else would go to such trouble, especially not someone for whom writing does not come easy. Besides, it's interesting, isn't it? From a medical point of view."

"I'm not a doctor," said Hanako.

"In some way we all are. Being a doctor is contagious."

"Perish the thought!" Yukiko rubbed her hands together. "Praised be the eternal light."

"So how long will it be before he realizes something's not right with the toy?" asked Hanako. "Not that I really care ..."

"I don't exactly watch him," said Sachiko.

"You switch things around, don't you, one year it's a monkey in the bundle and next it's a princess."

"Monkeys, princesses, little frogs," said Sachiko. "The rest I replace one-to-one. And every other year I put in a pinwheel."

"That sure is complicated," warbled Yukiko, who suddenly seemed to think the whole business was a lot of fun. Sachiko, Hanako and Yukiko often spent hours and days in such conversations that led nowhere and which no one understood. They had nothing better to pass the time.

Sachiko and Hanako wondered in silence how to measure the progress and intensity of Shimamura's reaction to the swapped playthings, without being too blatant. The fact that officially no one but he knew there were toys hidden behind the Charcot posed a problem. And who wanted to spend all day spying through a peephole? Besides, how could a peephole be installed in such a thick door? And who could look inside Shimamura's head and who would want to? "*Diegedankensind-frei*" Sachiko quoted the German folk song about freedom of thought—another phrase that wouldn't get her very far as a tourist in Germany—to which Hanako simply said: "You silly girl." Both women gently shook their heads. Yukiko meanwhile had conjured a bag of konpeito candy from out of her sleeve and was eating it piecemeal without offering them any.

"You keep all your estate papers under the floor of the south room," Hanako said to Sachiko. "In Stepfather's pharmacology book."

"That's right. And you study them in secret."

Hanako and Sachiko laughed. Yukiko stuck a hailstone-sized candy in the one spot in her mouth where two molars still connected, and cracked it open. Then she called out "I hide everything in the west! Right here!" And she banged behind her on the planks of the veranda.

"Money," said Hanako, "slips of paper from the temple, and scopolamine. We look at it every day."

Now all three laughed.

"Who hides things in the east?" asked Hanako.

"Sei?"

They all laughed, and all said "Poor Sei." They sat for a while in silence, without moving, and enjoyed the sound of the wind and the song wafting over. Then Sachiko doled out a new round of soft drinks and came up with another subject for a lengthy conversation.

9

Jean-Martin Charcot, who ruled over the women's asylum La Salpêtrière, was the most famous neurologist in the world and probably also the most famous Parisian—there really was no limit to his renown. He looked like a Roman emperor, spoke ten languages, including German, and with a charming smile was delighted to accept all of Shimamura's woodcuts from Nagasaki as soon as he laid eyes on them. He explained they would enrich the planned second volume of his book *Les Démoniaques dans l'art*, which proved also to lay readers that female insanity and so-called possession were a universal phenomenon, historically as well as geographically. Then he quickly changed the subject.

Dr. Shimamura couldn't say why he found himself sitting at the table of Professor Charcot like an old family friend, just days after he finally discovered the asylum. He vaguely remembered a whole swarm of female patients buzzing around him the minute he stepped into the Salpêtrière, and that this swarm had immediately transported him to Charcot like bees carrying a queen.

Meanwhile Charcot's assistants had been swarming around the master. And he had been very busy, because every patient he visited on his evening rounds displayed some neurological disorder as soon as he approached the bed. The patients who were escorting Shimamura likewise displayed a variety of symptoms the moment they spotted Charcot. The result was a great hullabaloo. And in the middle of all this noise, among all the fluttering hair and flapping shirts, Charcot caught sight of Shimamura. And something happened. A spark leapt between them.

(Later, in the many versions of his memoirs which he wrote in German so Sachiko couldn't read them, he had to replace this very apt expression with "sympathy arose" even though it didn't accurately capture the moment. But Shimamura had so often made a mistake while writing the sentence and discovered that he'd put down "fox" instead of "spark" that he gave up on the latter).

Whatever it was that happened when Charcot caught sight of Shimamura and Shimamura caught sight of Charcot—it was there to stay. The shrine of neurology opened its doors, and the young man on the imperial stipend was soon sitting in Charcot's mansion on the Boulevard Saint-Germain, poking at truffled grouse and discussing the simple dignity of Noh theater, especially with the head of the household, who had been impressed by what he had seen at the Exposition Universelle.

Long before he fully understood the Salpêrrière, one thing was clear to Shimamura: Professor Charcot was quite fond of animals. He had a sign posted at the entrance to the clinic letting it be known that dogs were not experimented on there. The decapitation laboratory at the Sorbonne was a thorn in his side. Even guinea pigs elicited his sympathy. He owned a pet monkey who answered to the name Rosalie and was allowed free rein. He would stop beside a draft horse and speak to it consolingly. Shimamura's woodcuts set off a long tirade against the horrors of fox hunting, in which he was completely oblivious to the fact that his index finger was resting the entire time on a half-animal penis protruding disembodied from the folds of a kimono. Shimamura had to suppress a laugh. Then he was moved. Then he was hungry. Then he had a headache. Then he felt a chill. He took a deep breath. He still did not like looking at the foxes.

Also, for a long time after he learned that it derived from a former gunpowder factory, the name "Salpêtrière" bothered Shimamura: every time it came up he was afraid the patients would think of explosives, and that couldn't possibly be good for them. After the first evening, which he probably was misremembering anyway, he never again saw the fluttering shirts and hair. Appropriately corseted and clothed, the female patients were kept out of their beds during the day and set to work and given physical exercises; they ate at long tables in stone halls that looked the way a cloister probably did. At first glance they appeared amazingly healthy. In Tokyo, even in Matsue, the insane were much more insane. They also received more visitors. In Paris there was no one lamenting next to a pile of mussed up bedding, not a single aunt, sister, mother, or grandmother was praying, smoking and bringing food. Shimamura was still wondering how to explain such a difference when he learned that the women isolated here for examination all suffered only from hysteria. He had to hear it many times before he finally believed it. Charcot's teaching as well as his fame were founded on hysteria, which he had redefined, moving it from a gynecological sideshow to the center of the neurological stage, and freeing it from the suspicion of being nothing more than a bad doctor's excuse or a female patient's wickedness. The Salpêtrière, at least the visible part—because there were probably hidden wards with patients who were demented or catatonic or suffering from all kinds of hereditary afflictions and who received little medical relief—was the paradise of hysteria. So said Dr. Tourette. Then he repeated himself, going as far as calling it a "little garden of paradise." One could only marvel at it all.

"I have only diagnosed one case of hysteria," said Dr. Shimamura, as they were taking a break to eat a snack in the courtyard, and the sentence sounded heavy as the grave. So much so that when he uttered it Dr. Tourette seemed shocked. "It is a difficult diagnosis," Shimamura quickly added, "and I am a young, inexperienced physician." Dr. Tourette turned his face to the sun and said: "Yes, yes, and so on."

Charcot's assistants Tourette and Babinski took care of Shimamura when Charcot didn't have time for him, which at first was mostly the case. Dr. Tourette had studied mood disorders in the German army; Dr. Babinski was Polish. For these reasons, according to Charcot, both ought to have a command of German, and if not they ought to be ashamed of themselves. One day Charcot set his monkey, which he often took to work, on Tourette's shoulder and laughed heartily. Tourette and Babinski laughed along; after all Charcot was their teacher. In Tourette's case the laughter sounded pitiful; with Babinski it was jovial. Tourette was unkempt, lopsided and short: Babinski stood straight like an officer. For years Tourette had clung to a study of his own creation, concerning an absolutely atrocious variant of neuropsychiatric tic, while Babinski was content to wander in Charcot's broad footprints. All the female patients hated Tourette and loved Babinski. Shimamura, filled with compassion, tried to like Tourette, but was unsuccessful. In one of the few letters home he wrote out the full name of the French doctor: Georges Albert Édouard Brutus Gilles de la Tourette, and described the tic he was clinging to and which in reality was not a glorious disease.

German did not flow easily either from Tourette or Babinski.

Every day Shimamura sat in on Charcot as the famous doctor received dozens of cases in the large examination room—always careful to move his chair a little behind an assistant, usually Dr. Babinski, who seemed best suited as a protective shield, because he wanted to stay as far away from the female patients as possible. These were summoned and led in one at a time. Nurses removed parts of the patients' dresses to expose the hysterogenic zones, which seemed to encompass practically the entire female body, and at that time were still awaiting systemization. These zones were then observed by everyone and manipulated by one assistant or the other. There were patients who could be stuck in the arm or neck with a long needle so that it came out the other end and they didn't feel a thing. Others might fall into a state, start twitching or even present with paralysis as soon as their stomach or shoulder blade or finger was grazed with nothing but a feather. Some assistants used grease pencils to mark the zones in question with lines and circles. Others then recorded the lines and circles in their notebooks and added comments. Charcot sat on a large armchair, somewhat raised, far in the back behind Shimamura, and directed the goings-on. Rarely would he go up and actively do something himself. But once he grasped a young girl by the chin, whereupon she went stiff and seemed about to fall over, then she cried out and sank practically to her knees and started kissing Charcot's hands, which Shimamura found disgusting. If someone did that in Tokyo, he thought, she would be sent home right away on account of hysteria. There must be something beyond that here, if the case was of such interest. After many days observing, Shimamura knew all there was to know about the structure of French undergarments and nothing about the anatomy of Charcot's hysteria. He complained about this to Tourette and Babinski, but neither understood him, either because of Shimamura's politeness or because of the German language. Then he managed to collar Professor Charcot in the corridor. Dashing ahead, he sidestepped Dr. Binet, who unfortunately also worked in the Salpêtrière when he wasn't measuring reaction times at the Sorbonne, grabbed Charcot by the elbow, and said "my friend" before expressing his dissatisfaction. Now that the woodcuts were gone, Shimamura was forced to play the oriental card in this manner, by committing faux pas in the hope someone might be moved by them.

Luckily, Professor Charcot was very moved by faux pas. In less than an hour Charcot himself escorted Shimamura to the Photographic Services Department, to give his Japanese colleague a better explanation of hysteria.

The Photographic Services Department had at its disposal

a magnificent atelier with all the requisite darkrooms and labs. It was situated in a small tower with a cupola illuminated by enormous windows. Inside, a variety of tableaux had been constructed: a hospital bed with glossy black rails and much white bedding; an armchair similarly draped with white, atop a pedestal; a footstool on another pedestal that was piled high with mattresses and pillows to form an undulating landscape. And throughout the space more sheets had been skillfully hung as drapes and backdrops. A wide assortment of cameras waited on tripods to be deployed: regular cameras of the most expensive kind, stereoscopic cameras, and one with twelve lenses and quick-action release. Light flooded the room from overhead and all around. The light of reason, thought Shimamura, and then he felt a sudden dread and then anger. "Oh my!" the student cried out, delighted by all the fantastic cameras, and Shimamura saw him tipping over the cliff and gently spinning into the deep, with his white loincloth and his white bottom—"Oh, Sensei!" Shimamura wanted to stop his ears. But the voice wasn't coming from outside—"Oh! Oooh!" Shimamura regretted that he couldn't shut his brain. Instead he kept his mouth closed so that nothing wrong came out. "In this Atelier," said Charcot, "we photograph everything, just as it happens, so that nothing may be considered arbitrary."

"Might I ..." Shimamura cleared his throat. "Might I stay here a little and make some notes? Where such technology is concerned Japan is still in its infancy." Suddenly he no longer wished to have hysteria explained. But Charcot wasn't listening. He shooed some people away—a nurse, a half-naked patient whom they had photographed and were now trying to force back into her institutional clothes, evidently against her will, and Dr. Bourneville with an emesis basin full of negatives—and seated Shimamura in the white-draped armchair on the white-draped pedestal. Then he pulled a file out of a cabinet and placed it on Shimamura's knee. "Voilà," said Charcot. "Since you are a lover of art ..." and with the help of the photographs he proceeded to explain *la grande hystérie* as follows:

There were four distinct phases, always the same ones. Charcot's *grande hystérie* was a drama in four acts, a symphony in four movements. Charcot emphasized this over and over with different allegories, as he quickly leafed through the perfectly illuminated prodromal stages of several female patients that were less than fully representative.

Then he came to the first phase, which he called epileptoid, as presented by five women. Shimamura recognized all the settings, the bed with the black rail that was always beautifully placed, the footstool with the mattress landscape, the armchair on which he was sitting. Five limber bodies used these props in various ways to perform what they proceeded to perform. Whether epileptoid was the best word, Shimamura preferred not to judge. Tetany, contractions, grimaces, salivation, craning, rolling, clinging, gyrating, twitching. Not a single picture was blurry. Shimamura leafed through all five cases and each was a perfect example of the arch of hysteria, the head bending backwards, hands cramped into paws, the pelvis thrust upward. "Our famous arch," said Charcot, pausing for a moment to let the arch have its effect. In each image the drapery cast its beautiful, discreet shadow, the breasts were always barely covered, while all five women vaulted backwards, like fairground acrobats, like fish flapping on dry land, over pillows, blankets, bedrails, animated with interesting powers. "Paroxysm," said Shimamura. The word came out squashed and with a horrible Japanese accent, even accompanied by a slight snort. Shimamura again cleared his throat. Charcot gave him a censorious look, as if his guest had coughed during an opera. "Congratulations," said Shimamura, senselessly.

"We call the second phase *clownisme* because of the antics," Charcot explained. He pulled his watch out of his vest pocket and let it chime. "Turn the page."

Shimamura did so, and leafed through ten, then twenty illustrations of antics that could hardly be described as droll. Nor at first glance did they appear to exhibit any regularity. Charcot was explaining more and more rapidly, and Shimamura obediently ran through the pictures, also more and more rapidly. The *clownisme* phase gave way to the "grand movements" and then the "passionate attitudes"—and here appeared the backdrop with the footstool, mattress and pillows, the white waves good for rolling, kneeling, crawling. To accelerate the private tutorial, Charcot started underscoring his explanations with gestures, and soon he was doing a lively dance among the white sheets surrounding Shimamura's armchair. He imitated the patients, giggled, implored, enticed, in keeping with the photographed women, pulling his invisible long hair and then throwing his arms open, freezing as though crucified. "In phase three every contortion embodies a feeling, an idea," Charcot cried out. "Mockery! Annoyance! Love! Ecstasy! Religion! In no logical order!" Shimamura flipped more pages. Now the corset was open, the tongue sticking out. Charcot was perspiring. Now he was speaking increasingly in French. "*Passions! Passions!*" He let his tongue dangle from the left corner of his mouth, while winking with his right eye, and then clasped his hands to form a pyramid, moving them up and down in front of his stomach and appearing to recite the Lord's Prayer. Then he grabbed a pillow and used it to mime "love." Shimamura twisted this way and that on his white armchair so as not to miss anything. "*Tournez!*" said Charcot. Shimamura turned more pages. All sorts of voices, real and false, mixed inside his brain—the voices of the girls in the photographs, the voice of Charcot, his own voice shouting curses, and the voice of the Emperor, a solemn, sonorous voice that said: "Shimamura, we don't need this." And then the student. And the fishmonger's daughter. What was her name again? "*Paroxysme*," said Charcot. "Phase terminale." He cramped his hands into claws and then relaxed.

Dr. Shimamura looked around. Dr. Bourneville had entered, as had a lab technician. The nurse and her patient, who was still unlaced and flitting around with loose braids, had also come back and were circling the white pedestal. Because Shimamura wasn't turning pages, Professor Charcot struck a few more poses of the terminal phase to finish the presentation. He sniffed at his fingers and grabbed at something invisible. "*Délire.*" Shimamura leafed on. All five patients slumped on an armchair—the same white armchair where he was sitting. Three of them had lost their corsets. Charcot mimed that as well, as best he could. Now quiet, he purred little snippets of French. The nurse tugged the patient behind a screen. The stereoscopic camera wobbled. Dr. Bourneville was busy with an appointment calendar. Three more colleagues, including

Binet, had filtered into the Photographic Services Department and immediately took whatever seat they could find so as to calmly admire Charcot's demonstration of the *grande hystérie*. Professor Charcot caught one last butterfly. For her part, the patient behind the screen seemed inclined to fall directly into *clownisme*, quite against the rule, a wild shadow play. The women in the pictures were all collapsed. Shimamura's fingers clung firmly to the final photograph. Charcot was breathing heavily. A minor expiratory stridor. Once more he raised his arms, then let them drop slowly and finally stopped.

"Enough for today," said Charcot. He placed his hand on Shimamura's shoulder. Shimamura felt himself trembling. Charcot reached around, closed the portfolio, lifted it off Shimamura's knee and tied it lovingly shut.

"The lie …," Shimamura began.

The nurse pulled the patient out of the atelier. Bourneville led the technician into the darkroom. Binet and his two colleagues stood up and slipped off. It had started to rain; the dark drops beat against the windowpanes, all the bright glass.

"The lie …," Shimamura repeated.

Charcot put the file back in the cabinet.

"The lie is one part," said Professor Charcot, "an essential component of the *grande hystérie*." He stroked Shimamura's shoulder until Shimamura stopped trembling, all the while observing his colleague with interest. Shun'ichi Shimamura took far too long to get out of the armchair. And he was far too hesitant in following Charcot out of the atelier. Charcot wanted to dash down the stairs and sprint along the corridor to make up for all the lost time, but Shimamura could only move at a snail's pace. As his guest crept along, step by step through the Salpêtrière, Charcot courteously stayed by his side.

"I am inconsolable," said Shimamura, "and I am ashamed for myself and for my entire country, but I don't understand it, I do not understand your *grande hystérie*.

Charcot stopped. He turned to face Shimamura. An elderly gentleman, who wheezed when he breathed, who needed three matches to light a cigarette because his fingers were arthritic, smiled and said, "I don't understand it either," and then jauntily exhaled the smoke through his nose, "and that, too, is an essential component. How is it going by the way, the business with the fox?"

Charcot always brought up the fox whenever Shimamura wasn't feeling his best.

"A lie... That is also a lie," said Shimamura.

"Of course. But how does it work? Who is he? How does he get inside?"

"It's a she," Shimamura muttered.

"Oh?"

"She comes in through the nipples or crawls under the fingernails, or more rarely through the ear." Then in order to spoil Charcot's enjoyment Shimamura cried out "international hysterogenic zones!" Finally he explained in rather complicated, presumably incomprehensible words that the lack of gender in Japanese nouns was a sign of a highly mature, philosophical language.

"Say something," Charcot suddenly requested. "I like hearing Japanese so much. So musical. So pure."

Shimamura was silent. He was now creeping along so slowly that they weren't making any progress at all.

"Don't you know a poem?" asked Charcot. He flicked away his cigarette, just like that, onto the floor of the corridor. Then he fished a new one out of his case, as Shimamura recited:

"The master of the powder factory
is up to his neck in foxes
which is why his breath whistles
and his fingers are stiff and why
he soon must go to rot and ruin."

"Aah," said Charcot. He waved his hand in the air as though he were conducting an orchestra.

"A poem on cherry blossoms," said Shimamura. "From Uji."

Just then a patient came their way, looked at Shimamura and fell stiff as a board at his feet. Then she began to rave. She raved fiercely, for two hours, and was not to be stopped, not by Charcot, not with laudanum, not with the straitjacket, not even when Shimamura swiftly removed himself. No clowning, no grand movements, no passionate gestures gave structure to her raving. She barked. She spat blood. She scratched her head until her fingers were sore, she scratched everyone's arms and hands, the walls, the floor. Professor Charcot, long after his guest had been escorted away, heard in her crying a foreign tongue and saw something looming and moving under her skin that was neither tendon nor muscle nor bone.

"Astounding," Charcot said to Babinski. "Let's bring our Japanese friend to the lecture. And then we'll send him home to Japan."

IO

"I've never forgiven you," said Shun'ichi Shimamura to Volume Six of the French Charcot, as he pulled it off the shelf so he could once again hold in his hands Kiyo's toys. He untied the bundle, then set the top spinning on his desk and, smiling, twirled the bamboo stick between his fingers to make the little monkey climb.

Thinking about Charcot always made him smile. His students at the Kyoto Prefectural Medical College had made a sport of suddenly saying "Charcot" whenever Professor Shimamura walked past, because it never failed to elicit a smile — the only smile in his repertoire: it even lifted his moustache. "Charcot, Charcot," the students would exclaim — and even in the middle of a lecture this would force a smile from Shimamura — Shimamura the most lenient professor, the mildest examiner, the most gentle human being — and he would interrupt himself and address the class with "Eh, well, what about Charcot?" Then he would have one student recite Charcot's neurological triad for multiple sclerosis: nystagmus, intention tremor, and dysarthria, although the students could never figure out what was so smile-worthy about that.

"I can never remember exactly what toys are in this bundle," Shimamura muttered to himself. "There's bound to be a reason for that and I ought to make a note." He reached into the pocket of his robe and took out the notebook where he jotted occasional ideas for the memory project. The notebook seemed as unfamiliar as the toy. Had it always been brown? He stuck it back in his pocket.

Then he laid the toys on the crumpled cloth, which he carefully tied back into a bundle and crammed onto the shelf. "There you go, you old arthritic liar, you've been dead now for a long time," Shimamura said to Volume Six of the French Charcot, sliding him back into the row of books so that everything was nice and tidy.

Ever since Shimamura, confused and flattered, had assured Charcot that he would be happy to assist with a lecture at any time, the professor had once again made himself scarce. And once again Shimamura saw himself running up and down the Salpêtrière behind Babinski, chasing after information. "Look it up, it's all in the books," said Dr. Babinski, who seemed unable to comprehend that someone might not understand French. The Salpêtrière was packed with Charcot's works; the myriad volumes in multiple copies took up yards and yards of bookshelves. Was it the will of the Imperial Commission that Shimamura learn French? He kept studying the books from the outside as well as from the inside, without result. "What is your therapeutic practice?" he asked Babinski more than once and Babinski answered "Rest, laudanum, cold water, look it up." And with that he sighed, as if only a philistine, only a simpleminded oriental would want to destroy the artistic masterpiece of a *grande hystérie*.

The days until Tuesday, when Charcot's next lecture was scheduled, passed slowly. With a tinge of rebellion Shimamura assisted Dr. Binet, who without Charcot's knowledge was measuring reaction times of the female patients with a pocket tachistoscope. His free time he spent going up and down the boulevards. He would turn up his collar, pull his hat down into his face and walk quickly ahead, bent forward as though fighting a wind, in order to avoid encounters. Half aghast and half with a diagnostic eye he observed the swaying silhouettes of the ladies, their martial steps, their long, soft arms slung around purchases, umbrellas and little dogs, the arabesques of their scarves, their hats. At home, when he ventured out of his room, the law students called out "*hisuterii*" and made all sorts of mischief. If only he had never mentioned the word. He went with them to the Cabaret of Hell and got drunk.

At last it was Tuesday.

Running a temperature of over 100 degrees, Shun'ichi Shimamura made his way to the Salpêtrière. The tram was packed. Hackneys were pulling up to the gate. People were pushing into the entrance hall. So at last they have a visiting day, Shimamura thought, somewhat leery. He went to report to Dr. Tourette as he had been instructed.

"Today is your day," Tourette snapped. He didn't invite Shimamura into his room and instead maneuvered him past the crowd, then guided him through a narrow door into a dark hallway where some old equipment was stored: a kind of padded harness with straps and screws and a threaded axle, an entire arsenal of the devices. "Special passage to stage," said Tourette. "Ovary compressors. Discarded. Unreliable stimulus. Just like you."

"Pardon?" said Shimamura.

The corridor led directly to the main auditorium and a rear entrance onto the stage.

"Rabbit," said Tourette. "Hat. Not everyone wants to see beforehand. Do we understand? Thank you."

"I ... *pardon*?" asked Shimamura.

Without a word, Tourette shoved him onto a stool located behind a masking screen at the edge of the stage. "Don't move. Until Charcot. Or I. Thank you." And he was off.

Shimamura peered through a crack between two panels of the screen. The amphitheater was large, with considerable brown wood and pear-shaped lamps. The rows were already well filled. Men in black, men in gray, ladies with feathered hats, once more the figures in the outmoded robes who Shimamura thought were poets, Dr. Beaunis with some students and the people from the guinea pig lab, Charcot's daughter with her husband, and very far in the front a large woman in moss green next to a boy in a sailor suit. Shimamura understood that neurology was being taught to the public, and suppressed his own opinion on the matter. The child in the sailor suit seemed familiar. Perhaps Shimamura had seen him in the morgue with the bodies from the Seine. Maybe the green lady wasn't his mother but his teacher. Was that important? Wise? Did Japan have to know that? Shimamura couldn't concentrate on any of this because his overheated brain kept droning the words "rabbit" and "hat" and nothing else. But he found no association, no saying, no image, no allegory. The question of what Shimamura had in common with an ovary compressor paled against this problem. Rabbit? Hat? Was Tourette's German so atrocious? Or was he simply trying to annoy Shimamura? Ever since Charcot had given him a personal demonstration of the stages of hysteria, Tourette had treated the guest with scarcely concealed disdain.

More and more people crowded into the hall. All the seats were long since taken. Is it possible Charcot was charging an entrance fee? Did he divvy up the proceeds among his patients, so they could buy frills and trinkets, the compassionate Professor Charcot? For Emperor and Fatherland, Shimamura thought crossly. And then it all began.

Charcot spoke a few words of welcome. Then Babinski led in a little man suffering from Parkinson's disease. The man was obliged to shuffle around on the dais and manifest the major symptoms. Charcot brought a device for measuring the tremors. Finally Dr. Bourneville applied small electrical shocks to his back and chest. The little man was so embarrassed that he didn't react to anything. He was supposed to say something, but he didn't. Charcot's charms were wasted on the sick man. The audience was audibly bored. The boy in the sailor suit tried to chew his nails and the green woman gave him a slap. Then she took some notes. Perhaps she was studying neurology here in secret, Shimamura suddenly thought, in order to commit a crime. He ruminated on this a while, but no crime occurred to him that required the study of neurology. He was so preoccupied with that thought that he missed the first case of hysteria. It wasn't until the second case that he again peered through the crack.

The woman was already half naked. The audience sighed. As expected, the focus was on hysterogenic zones. The neck. The lips. The palms. The upper abdomen. Next would have come the lower abdomen, but this was not demonstrated, only explained. Soon it was time for number three, a tender young thing with chestnut-brown braids that Charcot gently brushed aside to stimulate the earlobes, first with feathers and then with needles. Even the nurse who helped with the undergarments was pretty, the only pretty nurse in the whole damned Salpêtrière. Before he knew it the fourth patient was on stage, trembling. With a glassy gaze she stretched out her long, beautiful tongue toward a tuning fork. Oh what an apeshow of anguished sexuality, Shimamura formulated carefully in his mind, in German. He felt a sense of elation. The longer he was in France, the better his German became. Suddenly the entire linguistic beauty from all the Reclam classics he had read as a student came to a creative coalescence inside his head. Gotthelf. Paul Heyse. Immermann. The sailor boy looked delighted as he stuck three fingers deep inside his mouth. The green woman was writing. Was she from the newspaper? A poet? Each one of the female patients swooned onto Babinski's broad chest, while Charcot was busy with their zones and Bourneville was handing off one apparatus after the next, and Tourette watched, all the while moving his lips. Perhaps he was hissing *"foutu cochon"* like the marquise whose tics had served as godmother to the famous malady that bore his name. The audience applauded as the nurse led the fourth hysterical patient away, and Tourette popped out of the floor right next to Shimamura's footstool, like the devil in a theater.

"Get ready. You're next," he said, and Shimamura spun around, taken aback by Tourette's use of the familiar *Du*. "And by the way, read the books," Tourette whispered with a sneer, "like Babinski says – perhaps German better?" His unpleasant mouth cracked an unpleasant grin. "That guest from Vienna, Freud. All lectures in German." Tourette spat these words out like spoiled food. He seemed to dislike the guest from Vienna as much as he did the guest from Tokyo. "So why are you telling me that only now …" whispered Shimamura. Then came a burst of applause, and Tourette again materialized in the center of the stage. "Pff," said Shimamura into the crack in the screen. He could have been reading for weeks. Understanding everything for weeks. He sighed. The applause swelled louder and louder, then suddenly broke off and gave way to a reverential silence.

A new patient had entered. Proud, heavy, shy, and insane, she stood in front of Charcot. Babinski and Tourette watched her furtively from both sides, as though she were a precious vase that might get knocked over at any moment. She was no longer young and hadn't been groomed or laced up, and her disheveled hair was thinning on top. She stood there in bare feet, her corpulent body draped with a sheet starched as stiff as a board. Otherwise she was wearing nothing. She swayed gently as though she were dizzy. With every movement the sheet wrinkled into geometric prisms. Charcot addressed the audience. He, too, swayed slightly, as though he and the afflicted woman were standing on board a ship. I don't want to do this, thought Shimamura. I don't want to go out there. Bourneville had stepped up and was passing a Helmholtz ophthalmoscope back and forth in front of the patient's face, chanting numbers as he did. Charcot looked intensely in the other direction. Shimamura stared at the ophthalmoscope. Mesmerism? Hypnotism? Was he serious? Oh *pfui*, Professor Charcot. Two tears rolled down the patient's cheeks, and then her eyes slowly closed. *Rabbit ... hat ...* kept droning inside Shimamura's brain. The patient was long since cataleptic, her hands folded into the sheet, her blue eyes like glass. Shimamura tried to swallow but couldn't. Bourneville slipped the ophthalmoscope back into his vest pocket and stepped away to join Babinski and Tourette.

Charcot spoke to the audience as he gently pulled the patient's right arm out of the fabric and lifted it, then bent it and shaped it into an expressive pose. The ship on which they were standing was no longer rocking, it had docked and now Charcot's companion waved weakly over the railing. He touched her chin. Her head moved to the side. He reached into the sheet. Her body folded over at the waist. Charcot spoke, and as he did he tenderly bent each finger of the waving hand—but backwards. Her hands were broad and pale, with inflamed nail beds. Under Charcot's touch, one hand was transformed into some sort of bizarre growth that did not belong on a human arm. "*Bienvenue Nagasaki*," Charcot purred. And then Shimamura was standing in the middle of the podium with no idea how he had arrived there.

The blue eyes of the somnambulant woman were peering straight through him. Her lips were slightly open. He could feel and smell her breath, a gentle whiff of lemon balm tea.

Then he felt Charcot's index finger in his back. He walked slowly backwards. The patient came too, swaying, one little step at a time, like a caterpillar lifting itself at the edge of a leaf, feeling its way. The deformed hand relaxed. She fished an umbrella out of the air, which she used to ward off the snow. Her head, too heavy for her neck, jerked and pecked like a pigeon's. She shielded herself against the sun. Against the snow. Against the sun. Then the umbrella slipped out of her hands and she stood still, a white triangle with asymmetries as complicated as a woman's soul, as complex as the love of the bamboo princess who sinks at the feet of the emperor under a full moon. And there, sinking down, she kowtowed on the floor. Shimamura, his neck throbbing, backed off. The bamboo princess, swathed in her moonlit hair, hid her face in a sleeve, then in a fan. Sounds came from her mouth, first a cooing, then a gasping, then words. Her hair grazed Shimamura's shoes, and then she was drawn upward as though by threads; she reared up, bent over, and sang. A foreign language that Shimamura understood. *Life, a turning wheel! Life, the wheel of pain!* She stretched out her arms. The spirit of the Lady Rokujo, trapped in the body of the Lady Aoi. *Life, fleeting as foam, broken on the wheel of those reborn!* A voice of lamentation, up and down, warbling, roaring, then a cry. *Brittle, brittle is life!* The black hole of her mouth. Many spirits were trapped in the body of Lady Aoi; one person alone could not have all these voices. *I am a shadow!* Now she plucked away at an instrument. Shimamura saw the smooth wood, the strings, the crescent holes in the sound board, the charms dangling from the tuning pegs. He dug his fingernails into his palms. The rail separating the stage from the auditorium pressed against his lower back. It was impossible to retreat any further. *Brittle! Brittle! Leaf of the banana tree!* She bowed deeply and the instrument blew away from her hands. Now she was once again crawling and feeling her way. Shimamura pressed against the rail. Their eyes met. She was awake, wide awake. Was that a smile? With two fingers she cautiously creased new pleats of madness in her stiff white garment. Then she sank lifelessly to the floor. And was reborn. There she stood, fresh and pure and embarrassed, a little girl in a spring dress fumbling with her sash who didn't know what to do with her fan. Or was she holding a small cup? A flower? A stuffed monkey? "Charcot," Shimamura whispered. He no longer saw the famous professor. Instead he saw plum blossoms in the first night of their flowering. And she was feeling her way through the trees. So young. So sweet. Was she blind? She reached out into empty space. Her puppetlike joints clicked gently. *There, the Umeda bridge ...* The rods manipulating Shimamura's paper arms slowly rose. *It is the bridge, beloved, that the magpies laid across the milky way ...* "Charcot!" Shimamura whimpered. *Here in the Tenjin woods is where we'll die. Namu amida butsu.* Shimamura withdrew the dagger from her bosom. Her body, a wisp, a trace—lifeless she sank at his feet. *Husband and wife for all eternity.* And he slit his throat. The audience went wild.

"Thank you," said Professor Charcot. Then Tourette took over. He shoved Shimamura across the stage and back behind the screen. Bourneville and Babinski hurried to help the patient. A wet washcloth, a vial of smelling salts were discreetly put into service. Something was still clicking. Shimamura realized it was Tourette snapping his fingers right in his face. "How dare you!" whispered Shimamura. He plopped onto his stool. And there he sat, perfectly still, as Charcot recited a long epilogue and the audience went silent, then applauded, stood up, chatting as they slowly left the room, as Tourette slinked away and Babinski marched past, as Bourneville secured his apparatus with the help of an assistant, as someone came with a broom to sweep the floor. Then he stood up. He was now alone in the grand auditorium of the Salpêtrière. He found the hallway with the ovary compressors and followed it, still a bit unsure of himself, but resolute and awake. He made his way to Charcot's consulting room. Patients ducked out of his way. A staircase, a corridor. Without knocking he stepped into the professor's room, and there was Charcot, still somewhat flushed and breathless, while his assistants hovered around him, engaged in an animated discussion. The blonde patient had had her hair tied up and was now wearing a green blanket over her sheet. She was leaning on Charcot's desk, still quaking like an aspen and talking with Babinski.

"Charcot," Shimamura hissed. Everyone turned to face him. The patient curtsied, like a child confronted by a scary stranger. "Thank you, thank you!" Charcot called out, grabbing both of Shimamura's hands and giving them a friendly squeeze.

"You showed her my woodcuts," said Shimamura. "You were with her at the Exposition. You are a deceiver. A swindler. An impostor, a rascal, a lying rogue, a charlatan." An entire German thesaurus came gushing out of Shimamura's narrow lips. "You are a disgrace," said Shimamura, "to the entire neurological profession. You ... you ... showman!" His neck was throbbing. The thesaurus ran out. "Scoundrel!" hissed Shun'ichi Shimamura, then bowed deeply and rose up and began to howl. The howl was the last thing he heard.

When he awoke he was lying on the floor with his shirt in tatters and his head nestled in the blonde patient's lap. Charcot, Babinski, Tourette and half a dozen other doctors were bending over him. Charcot's shirt was also torn. A bruise was forming over his left eye. He was beaming. The patient was stroking Shimamura's hair, which was standing on end.

The consultation room was devastated. Potted plants had been uprooted. The floor was littered with books, paper, writing utensils, percussion hammers. Chairs had been over-turned and a glass cabinet had been shattered.

Charcot and his patient calmly helped Shimamura to his feet and led him to the chaise longue. Babinski brought water. Tourette—pale with disgust—handed him a handkerchief.

"Better? Better? Better?" Charcot asked, concerned. He was still beaming.

"Better? Better?" aped the blonde patient.

Shimamura nodded. He tasted blood in his mouth. He swallowed and drank some water. Charcot had again gripped his hand and was stroking one of his forearms; the blonde patient stroked the other.

"My dear colleague," said Charcot, beaming so much it lit up the room. "That was the most well-ordered, most beau-tiful, detailed *grande hystérie* I have ever witnessed in a man. You have no idea how important that is. For neurology. For me. For everyone—whether lay person or physician. For all women in this bigoted world! For years I have been fighting the prejudice that the stronger sex is immune to this disease. I thank you. As a colleague. As a comrade-in-arms. Together we will prove to the world—"

"*Oui, oui!*" the patient shouted. "Prejudice!" Whereupon the Japanese man again lost consciousness.

Shun'ichi Shimamura fled Paris like a thief in the night. He ached in every fiber of his body. In his trunk he was carrying every single volume of the German Charcot, which he had been pilfering from the Salpêtrière whenever and however he could.

Le Temps ran an article that made brief mention of his appearance at the Tuesday lecture. The law students were so delighted they didn't even notice their companion had moved out until much later. Each of them bought at least five copies of the newspaper to mail to Tokyo so the article could be circulated there. Since no name was listed, they wrote in the margin: *The man in question is the psychiatrist Shun'ichi Shimamura, a student of Hajime Sakaki!* The scandal was kept in bounds.

As soon as he was on the train, Dr. Shimamura began reading Charcot. He lost track of time. It wasn't easy for him to admit it, but judging from his writing, Jean-Martin Charcot was truly the best neurologist in the world.

11

"Berlin," said Dr. Shimamura, "was ruled by nothing if not reason."

He stuffed his kimono sleeves up into his housecoat cuffs, which had acquired a new stain the day before: scopolamine and blood in the middle of a fleur-de-lis. It was April and icy cold. Good thing he had a warm robe, even if it was dirty and even if the women grumbled about it.

"Everyone spoke German," he went on. "I learned nothing but useful things. No one apart from me was suffering from hysteria. And I had an apartment all to myself, on Hannover-sche Strasse, within walking distance to the Charité. Nothing but medical research and plain old reason. And now stay here, Fräulein Sei, together with your ridiculous bucket."

The housemaid lowered her eyes and covered her face with her hands.

"Just sit down over there and keep me company." Shimamura pointed to the rattan chair. The trick was to catch her off guard. Then she couldn't refuse. Was she even capable of speaking?

"Now," said Shimamura.

She planted herself in front of the chair and again shut her eyes.

"Sit down," said Shimamura. "Meaning: bend in the middle and press your bottom onto the cushion."

It took effort but she obeyed. Back in Kyoto she had sat in chairs all the time, in the nurses' lounge. Or was that in the common room of the women's chronic ward?

"In Berlin," said Shimamura, "where I spent an entire year or maybe even two, I wrote dozens of articles in my spare time, about why Japan is good for the nerves. Pungent squatting, old radish for breakfast, a language with no grammatical gender or plural forms, houses so light they can fly away, family trees, family bathtubs, eight million gods, earthquakes, tsunamis, et cetera. All of that steels the nerves, I argued, and managed to weave in a lot of medical knowledge. Those were fun articles. I toyed with the idea of sending them off to *Kladderadatsch*, which is a magazine in Berlin. In the end I wound up sending them to the stove. I was never funny, Luise. Funniness is not part of my constitution. I learned everything there was to know about neurological electrodiagnosis and stage four syphilis. I dissected many brains. I bought this housecoat and wore it and I put on my Egyptian fez and that was my thirtieth birthday. Now and then, when the fever rose, my disease curled up into a ball under the skin of my stomach so that it almost felt like a hernia. Only rarely did I feel the fox head. At times I even felt the distinctive features of Professor Charcot. I was sorry to learn he had died. I missed him, along with his fat kabuki-princess. Because you know—of course you don't know: hysterics always seek out excess. Professor Mendel gave me a moment of hope: he used to ride on horseback alongside a streetcar, distributing alms from a basket. He also managed to establish a few asylums—all of them small—in Pankow. I thought I might find something for me, there with Mendel, but he just put me to work on brains. I warmed them in an incubator and injected Gerlach's carmine mass into gelatin. Professor Mendel wanted to find out everything possible about blood supply to the pons and cerebral peduncles. So I incubated and stained, incubated and stained, incubated and stained. It was astounding how many brains the Charité had stowed away, and how generous they were with them. I'm certain that I went through more than would fill an entire lecture hall. My dreams were taken over by dancing, carmine-stained oculomotor nuclei. Professor Mendel was pleased with my work. He always seemed to wonder about me, as if he couldn't quite get over the fact that someone who looked like me was actually a physician. But I was allowed to publish everything in the *Neurologisches Zentralblatt*. And I reported it all to the imperial commission. Because that was important for the future of Japan, wasn't it? Where would we be today without Gerlach stains of the cerebral peduncles? How old-fashioned, superstitious, and crazy would we still be—especially you, Anna-Luise—if whole cohorts of us hadn't gone out into the world and investigated for example how Professor Mendel of Berlin was staining his brains? Nothing but a tangle of scattered, earthquaking islands. Feel free to pull your legs up and sit on your little duck feet if that's more comfortable—after all, no one can escape his own skin. If I wasn't dissecting brains for Mendel, I was examining the laundress Jäger for Professor von Leyden—a laundress is someone who cleans and irons clothes for a living. Frau Jäger was a young woman whose right leg started tingling one day. I still think of it every now and then. She was the least insane person I've ever known, with the exception of my wife. She wound up in the neurological department of the Charité. She felt pins and needles in both the right leg and the left, then she could no longer get out of bed and could no longer hold her urine. She had gone walking on wet snow. Professor von Leyden handed her over to me. So I examined Frau Jäger. Every day I tested the faradic irritability of her muscles. And that went on for an entire year. For one whole year that ironing woman was dying of an ascending neuritis of the lower extremities, which developed into myelitis. Wet snow. One can only marvel. I documented everything meticulously. 'Well done, well done, Shimamura,' said Professor von Leyden. I kept coming in with my galvanic apparatus. Frau Jäger thought I was Chinese. And so every day I said 'here comes the Chinaman with the electricity, Frau Jäger,' and Frau Jäger would say 'oh no, no.' She didn't say much else. She had two small children. To them she said: 'Be good.' Von Leyden kept bringing Frau Jäger to the lecture hall. A handful of students. No applause. Necrotic bedsores and pulmonary edema. A lost cause. Frau Jäger mouthed the words 'oh no, no' and that was her thirtieth birthday. I eagerly waited for her to die. Then I autopsied her. Hers is the only brain from Berlin I can still picture, the gray degeneration of the posterior funiculus and plaques in the dura spinalis. Martha Jäger. The spotty degeneration of her lateral corticospinal tract. Her delicate, ischemic pia. Professor von Leyden allowed me to publish the case in the *Zeitschrift für klinische Medizin*. And I also reported it to the imperial commission. As I said, Berlin was ruled by nothing if not reason."

At this point Shimamura gasped a little for breath. He sat on the edge of the bed and stared at his feet. The Japanese house shoes made a fork in the European socks. Two pitiful, gray, crumpled cloven hooves on an oriental rug. They looked like pigs' trotters. Shimamura removed both slippers and socks and placed his feet in the bucket of water. As he did this he watched the housemaid. Had he finally guessed the purpose of her bucket? The girl kept a straight face. And why girl? She had to be at least thirty. For some time she'd been trying to tame her large breasts with the sash she used to tie back her sleeves. That didn't look good. Also she was so short. When she sat in the rattan chair her feet barely touched the floor. Shimamura wondered what her brain might look like. Probably fresh and healthy, full of joie-de-vivre.

"This is an impolite question," said Shimamura, "but tell me one thing, Luise: what do you find so likeable in me?"

It was simply impossible to call her Fräulein Sei. She continued to keep a straight face and didn't answer. Shimamura could understand that.

"Who are you anyway?" he asked. "Where do you come from? How did you wind up in the infirmary? Does my wife treat you well? And can you speak? Please say yes if you can."

A wrinkle formed between her eyes.

"Do I actually speak Japanese," Shimamura asked, "or do I speak German all the time?"

Her forehead smoothed out. Then she said "half-half." Her voice was strong and deep, almost like a man's.

"You sound different when you sing." That came out in Japanese.

She did not react.

"Will you sing your song for me?"

No answer. No song.

"May I go on with my story?"

Not a word. Perhaps she only spoke once a day, and now that was over.

"Thank you," said Shimamura. He lifted his feet out of the icy water, dried them on the bed cover and studied them. White and a little blue. What ugly feet. The housemaid had now lifted her own feet onto the chair and was sitting curled up like an animal. Shun'ichi Shimamura continued.

"I attended lectures on pathological anatomy with Virchow and in Dalldorf I drew pictures of beds, in particular of the padded straps that could be used to immobilize patients and which could be quickly slid under the mattress when not in use, so that at first glance the place didn't look so much like a madhouse. Professor Jully lectured on neurotic hypochondria at the Charité, while Professor Moeli lectured on crime and insanity at the Herzberge asylum. That was all very enlightening. But I preferred drawing the washrooms. I sketched the strangest things in Berlin, even sewers and a city rail signal tower. Unfortunately photography had been ruined for me. I believe I traveled as far as Halle, Jena, Dresden, Heidelberg in order to sketch everything there that was important, but I don't remember, and the drawings are most likely lost. There are two things in particular, Luise, which I can't remember: things that frighten me and things that bore me. In other words nearly everything. And what I forget faster than anything else is what's supposed to go into my book on memory, because that scares and bores me at the same time. What I do remember from that period is the Berlin women on the roofs at night. They sat there and meowed, or whatever else one might call it. Perhaps their skin was a little darker because the brown coal spoiled everything, but otherwise it was just like at home. I always wanted to go up and visit them when I looked out of my window on Hannoversche Strasse and heard them barking, snarling, hissing. Fortunately I refrained from doing so. Am I speaking German again? On the subject of dreams and animals: did you know that after mating, foxes can't separate for half an hour? That's called 'copulatory tying.' The male has long since finished and is looking in the other direction, but he's still stuck firmly in the vixen. Both flap their tails off to the side and act as if none of it mattered to them. For a whole half hour! I'm not surprised that this particular behavior hasn't found its way into folklore. It's simply *unromantisch*. Pardon the German adjective. It reminds one of water beetles and late summer dragonflies flying around stuck inside each other with the same indifference. Where did I leave off? Berlin? For a while I tried growing a Van Dyke beard, with a sad result. Feelings of inferiority. Pardon the technological term. My German colleagues on the other hand—now those were impressive beards! With my fuzzy bit of moustache I studied a case of myasthenia gravis and reported on that to the imperial—"

"That's enough, dear," said Sachiko.

The housemaid jumped out of the chair and the retired

professor was so startled he scurried into his bed, all the way under the covers. No one had heard Sachiko coming. Everyone knew she was able to appear out of thin air. But they always forgot.

"You're tiring yourself out, dear," said Sachiko Shimamura. The housemaid knelt down then jumped back up on her feet and dashed out through the open door, strangely bent forward, almost like an ape.

"Now you've made her completely mad," Sachiko stated. "She's even forgetting how to walk."

Shimamura slowly emerged from under the covers.

"What is it you're after with that bucket? Why does she have to bring it to you every day?"

Shimamura thought for a moment. Then he said: "change of pace."

Sachiko smiled and touched the bucket with the tips of her toes. Outside, by the quince trees, the housemaid was singing her song, as though nothing had happened. "In the tall grass, in the short grass, in Uji and Kei …"

"Like before," said Sachiko. "Isn't that so, dear?"

12

The daughter of the landlady who in the winter of 1893 rented a mezzanine room in the Hahngasse to Shun'ichi Shimamura had the idea of dressing him up as Molière's Imaginary Invalid.

It was the Fasching carnival season, and a Japanese painting student had invited Shimamura to an artist's ball. He had shoved a ticket in Shimamura's hand at the café where the stipend-holders regularly met. Shimamura had stuck the ticket on the shade of his desk lamp and that's where the landlady's daughter had discovered it. Her name was Barbara, she was studying acting, and often sat chitchatting on Shimamura's bed for long periods.

The Imaginary Invalid was not her first choice. She would have preferred to costume the Japanese man as a Japanese man, but she couldn't find a single thread of Japanese attire in Dr. Shimamura's luggage. So she pressed him to filch a large enema syringe from the hospital where he was now observing, to use as a prop for teasing the women, since that was the thing to do during Fasching. But no enema syringe was to be found at the Bründlfeld asylum, so Shimamura borrowed the bottom half of a device for measuring tremors. In spite of the beautiful case, Barbara wasn't content, and she spent several evenings experimenting on Shimamura with different makeup—chalk-white and bluish and red around the eyes—to compensate for the missing enema, until she finally created a mask that met her approval. One of her grandmother's sleeping caps, her deceased father's Turkish slippers, and Shimamura's own old-fashioned housecoat completed the costume. Shimamura was to keep his private thermometer jauntily tucked behind his ear, just like the carriage drivers kept their cigarettes. As she waited excitedly for the ball, Barbara put the finishing touches on her own elf costume. When the evening finally arrived, Shimamura let himself be made up and dressed, stuck the thermometer behind his ear and the tremograph under his arm, then pulled on a coat and disappeared into the night. Only hours later, when all the girls in the ballroom were whirring around him, did it occur to him he should have taken Barbara. But by then it was too late and their friendship never recovered.

Unsurprisingly, Shimamura didn't recognize anyone at the ball, not even the Japanese painter. The room was large, crowded, loud, and decorated with all sorts of ugly things— garishly colored tattered paper and old rubbish, including kitchen utensils and shoes—evidently an important part of the tradition. Shimamura started drinking—ever since Berlin he drank frequently, and on occasion quite a bit—and tried to recall where this particular holiday fit in the Christian calendar, so he might have a clue as to the sense of the evening— but he couldn't remember.

A number of women desired to make his acquaintance. Most of all they wanted to dance with him. The first waltz brought tears to his eyes, as it inevitably did in the opening measures, but the tears blended in well with the greasepaint and couldn't be seen. He managed to subdue the urge to stick the thermometer in his mouth or under his arm, and anyway he lost the thermometer early on. He didn't dance, because he didn't know how, but he did clink many glasses with many women. He let himself be questioned and fingered — his sleeping cap, his robe, the faux snakeskin case. Shimamura didn't want to unpack the actual device and risk damaging it. But at one point he did dance and at one point he did unpack the device and even tried to measure a female quiver, but all he had was the bottom half, which alone was useless. Shimamura felt ill and then he felt better and better, the more he drank.

The hours passed loudly. They had come to the closing polonaise. Now he could go home, thought Shimamura. Then he saw a girl who was costumed as a fish or a mermaid stumble during the polonaise. She collapsed and did not get back up. For a few measures she jerked around on her knees, and then tipped over onto her side. The dancers ruthlessly closed the gap. The girl put her head between her arms, then clutched her ears and began twitching. Large green scales started dropping from her costume and her crown of shells fell from her black hair. Someone bent over her and she kicked him. Then she started rolling over and over. And hitting and kicking. Shimamura entrusted the tremor half-device to his most drunken companion at the table, who was not in a position to make off with it, and crossed to the dance floor. He pushed through the dancers, observed the jerking fish for a while from above but couldn't figure it out. The kicking was too systematic for an epileptic fit. Expressiveness too slight for hysteria, and the famous arch was completely absent. Whatever she was shouting, assuming she was shouting and not simply gasping for air, was drowned out by the polonaise. She needs water immediately, Shimamura thought, as he wiped the drunkenness out of his cerebrum—an exercise he had mastered well in Berlin. He shouted "I'm a doctor" and knelt down amid the scales and broken shells. At last the dancers ducked out of his way.

For a solid half hour he couldn't make head or tail of the twitching fish. Nothing medical came to mind. Water was knocked away, then greedily gulped down, then regurgitated and spat out. The third glass Shimamura poured on her face, which resulted in a nice left-facial paresis, although it really wasn't. Tight, stumbling pulse. Perioral pallor as in a child with scarlet fever. The girl attempted to crawl with her hands like a seal on its flippers. And finally—a bleating, barking sound came from deep in her belly. Someone called out: "The family is here!"

"I've got you," whispered Shimamura. A group of people were now standing behind him, not wearing costumes, upper-class, a young man with a square beard, a pale older man with a goatee, an angry matron in gray. They were all shouting "Franziska!" Franziska was barking desperately. "I beg your pardon," Shimamura said to the goatee, who was the closest, and his German came out a little oddly, "I humbly beseech you, this is not what it might seem, Herr Father of Franziska, not at all, I am a doctor," and then he started doing something with the girl that he feared looked like an open-mouth kiss.

Shimamura awoke on the floor in a neighboring room, having been stably laid on his side, with the sleeping cap between his teeth. He spat it out and sat up. Muted dance music in the ballroom, all decorations taken down, two flushed waitresses in the distance, and the man with the goatee sitting on a chair. "Where is your daughter?" asked Shun'ichi Shimamura. "And where is my tremograph?"

"Her mother took her home. Your what?" The man was bending over him. "I am not her father." That sounded relieved. "I am the family physician. Are you feeling better?"

"She has made a fine convalescence, I trust?" Shimamura's German was still hitting a snag.

"Your what, please?" the bearded man repeated. Then he started to explain about epilepsy and apologize rather clumsily for the sleeping cap gag. Shimamura asked the waitresses to search the ballroom for the tremor device. He noticed his left hand was twitching. Actually it was not so much a twitch as a waving and wagging he couldn't control. He tried to hold the one hand in check with the other, but it swiftly worked itself free.

"Is the girl convalesced?" asked Shimamura. "Shimamura. Pleased to meet you."

"Breuer," said the doctor. "She recovered, as soon as you …" He pointed to his lips, with some embarrassment.

"So what was wrong with her?" asked Shimamura.

"Blood pressure."

"Blood pressure?"

"Yes. No. Neurosis. By now she is back home in bed. She had snuck off to the ball. She is sixteen years old, the family…"

The waitresses came scurrying over with the tremograph. Shimamura took it, relieved, and sat down on the case without further ado, since there was no other chair in sight.

"I am not epileptic, Herr Doktor Breuer," said Shimamura. "Now I am going to head home in peace, and I thank you for your help and hope that in my unconscious state I did not somehow hit you."

"Can you stop doing that?" Half reproachfully, half fascinated, Breuer pointed to Shimamura's hand, which in the meantime was flapping up and down on his knee.

"Not at the moment. But in time without doubt."

"And you are…"

"Also a physician."

Shimamura stood up, but he felt dizzy and had to sit down again. He would have happily gone home, to examine the fish hand on his own. As a test he tried putting it inside the sleeping cap, but that was immediately tossed off. "Neurologist," said Shimamura. "Currently at Bründlfeld."

"I completely misconstrued the earlier scene," Dr. Breuer began, slowly. "Since I arrived, since your… since you… since Fräulein Franziska… I don't know how to put it, Herr…"

"Shimamura," said Shimamura. "From Tokyo."

"Tokyo," Dr. Breuer repeated, dumbfounded. All the riddles of the night seemed to come together in this one word. He went so far as to tug at his beard. Shimamura had to smile.

Unfortunately, however, his entire left arm was now waving in the air.

"What kind of neurosis?" he asked.

"A convergence of multiple stimuli," mumbled Dr. Breuer. "Fish, dance … running away from home …"

"Fish?"

"There was an incident with an aquarium … Tokyo?"

"If I hadn't covered my face with carnival makeup," Shimamura said softly, "I'm certain you would have immediately noticed my far eastern background and not have been so taken aback. Aquarium?"

"It's complicated," said Breuer. "An aquarium and her first menstruation. They became mixed up and lodged inside her head that way. I can't really tell you the entire case history. Earlier … when you … when I approached …"

Gradually Shimamura's shoulder began to hurt, and his drunkenness slowly started to return. He swallowed, then burped, then swallowed again.

"It was not a kiss," said Shimamura. "It's complicated, and you wouldn't believe me in any case. It's a trick, an old Japanese trick, a kind of purification—a medical one, of course, a neurological one, an oral, so to speak …"—and he burped again horribly.

"My god," said Dr. Breuer. He helped Shimamura to his feet. "My surgery is right around the corner. Let's go there, and I'll give you something to calm your spasms." He tried to lock Shimamura's dancing arm under his own, and when that didn't work, he held tightly onto the other. With his remaining hand he clutched the tremograph. Shimamura

burped, gasped, "not necessary" and panted "many thanks."
And so off they set. The streets were covered with gray snow
that had frozen over. Here and there stray carnival revelers
staggered through the night. It was icy cold. And slippery.
And Dr. Breuer's surgery was not exactly around the corner.
What a good man, thought Shimamura. He clung tightly to
Dr. Breuer's elbow.

Warmed up, treated to English tea and cakes, and thanks
to a dose of chloral hydrate freed from all afflictions, he sat
cross-legged on Dr. Breuer's chaise longue and told him a long
story, in which the words "I don't remember" made frequent
appearances.

13

After the ordeal with Fräulein Pappenheim, which though ten years back continued to plague him almost nightly in his dreams and with jumbled memories that appeared out of nowhere, Josef Breuer attempted to keep all patient consultations to a bare minimum, though without much success. He also attempted to steer clear of neurology, the medical school, and all types of hypnosis even if it just consisted of a monotone bedside patting of hands, as well as Dr. Freud. For better or worse, Breuer had finally given in to Freud's constant yammering—which had a hypnotic tinge of its own—that it was time to "shed light on the Pappenheim darkness" and enrich science with a book that would take the case as a point of departure and publically shed light on Freud's own exuberant ideas, which grew wilder and wilder every year. Now Pappenheim's hysteria not only appeared to Breuer in dreams but also on paper, and it had become impossible to avoid Freud, as long as this damned book wasn't ready.

Apart from his flourishing private practice on the Brand-stätte, fulfilling his duties as house physician to several good families abundantly blessed with daughters, and coping with Freud who kept dropping in to sit and smoke and talk, Dr. Breuer enjoyed his work with animals. Every time he thought he'd completely lost his faith in science, they helped him re-discover it. He had set up one room of his practice as a labora-tory and spent hours there inducing rotary vertigo in tadpoles and crawfish with a centrifuge, or severing the vestibuloco-chlear nerve of cats, so that they could sit calmly on spinning discs free of nystagmus. "You are interested in vertigo," Freud concluded. Breuer's only reply was to hand him a basket of deaf kittens for his daughter Mathilde.

Dr. Breuer didn't know why, but all his good resolutions about not talking with patients simply dissolved when faced with the crazy Japanese who had blown into his house one Fasching night. Nor did it stop at the first recitation. The Jap-anese man kept coming back, practically pestered by Breuer to continue his account. At first glance the diagnosis seemed easy (psychosis, demonamania), but then proved impossi-ble. The Japanese sat on the chaise longue, drinking tea with scarcely concealed revulsion, and talked. His German was perfect and at the same time sounded completely Japanese, which puzzled Breuer. Fascinated by his new acquaintance, who wasn't so much a patient as an odd sort of guest who seemed burdened by fate, Josef Breuer began to neglect cats, crawfish and the Pappenheim book. He left Franziska von W. to her parents and her neurosis, and let on he wasn't home whenever Freud stopped by. He did however begin to visit the Court Library. But no matter how long and hard he searched the shelves devoted to Oriental Studies, he found nothing about Japan, as if the country did not exist. With some trepidation he invited the Japanese to dinner; after all, no matter what might be wrong with him, he was also a colleague. Breuer's wife and two little daughters were very taken with the guest and soon fell into feverish frivolity. The Japanese spoke briefly about myelitis, then about Viennese architecture and Clemens Brentano. After that Breuer preferred to confine their meetings to his practice, where he tried to sort out the matter systematically:

Shun'ichi Shimamura or Shimamura Shun'ichi, thirty-two years old, of youthful, asthenic appearance, left arm displaying spasmodic chorea which subsided promptly after 0.5 g chloral hydrate administered p.o., with no neurological or internistic findings. Subject seemed at all times slightly heated, with the bright, shiny eyes and excited, frequent pulse of a consumptive; the thermometer however did not indicate fever, nor did pulmonary auscultation reveal any abnormalities. With the exception of a cretinous aunt he comes from a sound family, to wit from the city of Takasaki located in the Kozuke province, which following the land reform is part of the Gunma prefecture. To his own amazement Josef Breuer had no trouble memorizing all these words right away, whereas the names of his patients had always caused him difficulty.

Following a quiet, diligent childhood, the young man was sent to Tokyo to study something he understood fit the definition of "medicine." It is clear from his report, however, that either in place of such study or perhaps to augment it, he became apprenticed to an exorcist, who according to oriental custom cured the sick by casting out beings that cannot be adequately described

with Christian terms such as demon or even devil. In this ca-
pacity, and with a copy of Griesinger's Mental Pathology in his
trunk, which further confused the entire matter, Shimamura
was sent personally by the emperor, who evidently took a lively
interest in the activities of physician-exorcists, to a remote prov-
ince in order to "cure the fox." This "fox"—and here it was
clearly "fox" that was meant and not for instance "pox"—refers
to a disorder that is difficult to grasp. Rooted in the Shinto cult,
it predominantly affects women, above all in summer. A woman
"possessed by the fox" –or more precisely "bitten by the fox" as the
Japanese let me know with great amusement—displayed symp-
toms Shimamura described fully in the manner of an occidental
physician. Beyond this, however, she would be overcome by all
manner of vulpine manifestations up to and including complete
transformation into a vixen. The Japanese described this using
language that was alternatively sparse and flowery but which
was always sexually tinged, until all at once he claimed not to
remember a thing. Whereupon he resumed the description using
Charcotian concepts (arch, clownism).

Charcot's abrupt appearance in the far-eastern fairy tale
threw Dr. Breuer off track. Suddenly he had a hard time con-
centrating and struggled to suppress mental pictures with
particular associations—the kittens from his laboratory,
Fräulein Pappenheim, as well as the three little maids from
Gilbert and Sullivan's Mikado. Shimamura, who for an Oriental displayed amazing empathy, then surprised Breuer with
German copies of his medical exams and asked the Viennese
doctor to inspect them carefully. The papers appeared legiti-
mate. They did not drive away the mental pictures, but from
then on Dr. Breuer referred to Shimamura as "Herr Doktor"

to stress he was a colleague. He also observed shame manifestations in his own person.

A fox exorcist, Josef Breuer understood, was often referred to by the shamanistic concept of "receptacle" due to the fact that he received the foxes that were coaxed out of the possessed individual. Here again Breuer's thoughts became muddled: the word "receptacle," with its nasty, passive connotations, provoked strong feelings of disgust, which were immediately transferred onto his Japanese guest, as if someone dirty were sitting there on his chaise longue, with a bucket full of the excretions of diseased women. The combination of Charcotian terms and that damned Griesinger, whom the Japanese kept mentioning, only served to heighten this disgust, as though Breuer himself might be harboring foxes which in the course of his medical activities he had absorbed inadvertently or even with healing intent. To crown it all it occurred to him that in Baroque German such as Grimmelshausen the word "fox" colloquially referred to something regurgitated. For a moment Dr. Breuer was on the verge of asking his guest to leave. "I do not believe," the Japanese explained, "that I have a fox or foxes in my body—de facto, in natura, in persona, or in animale. But ever since that time I have the feeling that my inner self is not entirely my own." He then trained his physician's eye on Dr. Breuer, since the Viennese colleague was perspiring, and also his speech likely sounded constrained. Josef Breuer stood up to open the window. "I'd just like to let in a little air," he said, "it's stuffy, I'll open this up a bit to let some in." Shimamura's gaze became even more diagnostic.

The fox per se was not the central problem. Rather it seemed as though the Japanese viewed his fox—because that's how he put it, the longer the conversations went on, the more distinctly he referred to "my fox" as though it were a kind of pet, unmanageable but halfway loved—not merely as a burden, but also as an instrument for sharpening his diagnostic sensibilities and healing talent. He seemed more bothered by a different moment he remembered only vaguely or Breuer imagined perhaps not at all—and suspected this was the underlying root of the trauma. He was able to detect two protagonists: a young fox patient who was very pretty and at the same time very trying, who Shimamura referred to as K., and Shimamura's own assistant, a youthful shaman who had been assigned to him back in Tokyo. This assistant, who constantly talked and smoked and who seemed carefree and assertive in his sexual affect, elicited such a strong defensive reaction in Shimamura's subconscious that the latter could not even recall his name.

It seemed this assistant had easily outperformed Shimamura in many areas: he performed the exorcisms faster and the possessed individuals and their families often preferred him over his master. He could better withstand the heat and squalor, could cope better with the terrain, and was generally more robust and cheerful. Eventually the nameless youth—the mention of whom caused the Japanese to wrinkle his forehead and lose some of his command of German—won the upper hand in the case of the patient K., with whom he journeyed into a cultlike, childish, and probably also amorous dream world that Shimamura was not allowed to enter, perhaps because he was clinging to his Griesinger—however Griesinger got drawn into the matter—and because he was not as respected as an exorcist. Apparently things came to a scandalous head on top of a roof. "The student disappeared and was never found again," said Shimamura with a wrinkled brow. "May I now tell you about Professor Charcot?"

Here Dr. Breuer emphatically declined. He was after reminiscence, and when instead of reminiscing Shimamura volunteered an anecdote about Jean-Martin Charcot, Dr. Breuer took a Helmholtz ophthalmoscope from his vest pocket and asked if he might hypnotize his colleague. At that point the Japanese stood up and found an excuse to escape.

Nevertheless he showed up punctually for their next session. This time he was carrying a notebook. The emperor's mandarins or bigwigs who had supported his trip abroad were clearly interested in methods of traumatic suggestion, including the phenomenon of hysterical counter-will. In the meantime he had read Breuer's contributions published in the Viennese medical journals and now saw things somewhat more clearly. He asked Josef Breuer to convey his deep-felt greetings to his coauthor Freud, for having translated Charcot into such beautiful German, and thereby sparing himself, i.e. Shimamura, serious shame. With these words he eagerly opened his notebook.

At that point Dr. Breuer was somewhat speechless. He found the situation repellent. He was overcome by a curious, practically infantile exhilaration that Freud was going to enter the annals of Japanese history as some highly esteemed emancipator of shame or some other ridiculous title; at the same time he himself felt gripped by shame the moment the Japanese uttered the word "shame," which brought to mind the repulsive fox-transfer. Shun'ichi Shimamura or Shimamura Shun'ichi — the name refused to stick in Breuer's mind — was

by no means troublesome. In fact for an insane person he was
extremely well-bred and retiring, but Breuer found him more
taxing than any patient he had had in years. In addition, Shimamura's notebook had prompted an unsettling role reversal,
as though the Japanese were examining him and not the other
way around—as though he, Josef Breuer, had been sitting on
a roof in Japan, amorously confused and jealously angry, together with a fox-possessed half-naked geisha named K. and
an overly assertive and talented younger colleague, and had
thrust everything out of his memory so as to protect his own
sense of self. Meanwhile this roof, which Shimamura had only
mentioned in passing, had developed in Breuer's fantasy into
a highly picturesque oriental scene, with tiles, chrysanthe-
mums, and Moorish arches under a full moon. The mood
was by its very nature erotic, and at the same time conducive
to bloodlust. Dr. Breuer asked the Japanese to kindly pick up
the story where he had left off, at the roof, and put aside the
notebook for the time being. Shimamura obediently closed
his notebook and said "I don't remember." At that point Josef
Breuer insisted. And insisted. And insisted. And hypnotized
to the best of his ability, as far as this was possible, surreptitiously and without accessories. The Japanese smiled, then
stopped smiling, finally his hand began to twitch, this time
his right hand, and tears streamed down his stubborn face.

And so the truth came to light. A crime had indeed been
committed. The young assistant had fallen first from the roof,
then from the cliffs into the sea—still talking and flushed
from a sexual encounter with K.—and this was not an accident. In fact it was the worst possible outcome that the
cathartic method might reveal, for right there on Breuer's

chaise longue a murderer was sitting, amid tears of horror and relief, having reproduced the terrible scene of his deed, and this confession had brought about his recovery. Shimamura's hand was twitching less and less. His tears were drying up. He let out an enormous sigh. Once again Breuer stood up to open the window and stuck his head far outside. What was he bound to do? What was his moral, legal, medical duty? He felt an overwhelming desire to shout out the window, "Police, police," like the grandmother from a fairground puppet show. But he forced himself to remain calm. What did one know about Japan? What did one know about shamans? What law did they understand? Was it possible that the pupil actually belonged to the master, just like some tool or magic potion, and that he was permitted or even duty-bound to commit suicide if he surpassed his master? Had the deed induced trauma only because the Japanese had traveled to Europe, where he was confronted with European customs and European law, with Griesinger, Charcot, and Breuer? Really what did one know about Japan? Dr. Breuer, cooled by the fresh winter air, decided to sleep on the matter, perhaps try his luck in the Court Library one more time, before undertaking possible further steps. He closed the window and walked over to Shimamura, who was sitting on the chaise longue looking rather petrified, and gave his colleague a long and heartfelt handshake.

Josef Breuer did not undertake any steps. Nor did he visit the Court Library. Instead he ran to see Freud. Now he was finally ready to embark on the joint book that had become such an annoyance. Freud noticed that his erstwhile mentor was astoundingly convivial and full of creative energy. Freud asked if Breuer had received some good news, or perhaps had a breakthrough with his kittens. Breuer didn't answer, and inquired after Freud's health and the health of the entire family, as though he were the family physician. Amazed, Freud assured him that all were well. Then Breuer burst out laughing. Freud laughed along, since Josef Breuer had once been his teacher and he still felt some obligation. So they laughed for a while. Then Breuer said, "I recently cast out a fox spirit, and this wasn't a dream but actual therapy," and related the case of Shimamura. He left out quite a bit, actually everything— everything except Japan and the animal in Shimamura's body.

Dr. Shimamura stayed at Bründlfeld, observing. But because Dr. Freud was a gossip monger, Shimamura kept hearing the words "fox spirit" more and more often at the asylum. Students, orderlies, and even Professor Julius Wagner Ritter von Jauregg, whom Shimamura accompanied on his rounds and who was hardly known for his sense of humor, teased him about it. Shimamura didn't have much in the way of a response. "The analytic conversation as a healing method for traumatic hysteria," he wrote to the imperial commission, "is of little use for Japan, as it contradicts our sense of politeness, and besides it takes too long." He returned home to Tokyo in the fall of 1894.

14

Shortly after his return from Europe, Dr. Shimamura was transferred to Kyoto, which was undoubtedly an honor. He was certified to teach neurology and psychiatry at the Prefectural Medical College and soon was appointed director of the new University Neurological Clinic. He found he was well equipped for all these tasks. He continued to run a fever. He continued to feel the occasional protuberance in his abdomen, just under the skin, which resembled a hernia or perhaps not. He didn't see that this ought to pose any impediment to his career.

He was well-liked by his students, who particularly enjoyed his course on forensics, even though he had never studied that subject himself. To illustrate the methods and findings of forensic medicine he resorted to visual aids and long, gruesome stories which he related in great detail, and often with a smile so tiny it did not raise his moustache in the slightest. For hours, days, months and years on end he lectured on stab wounds and strangulation, on water in lungs and blood in brains, on toxicology and defensive lesions, on hair and skin under fingernails. In that course he only touched on psychiatry tangentially. When the court asked him for competency evaluations, after a quick perusal of the case he would invariably declare the person insane, while shaking his head as if to say: one never knows.

Since Professor Sakaki was no longer pressing him, his scientific work receded further and further into the background. For a while he tried to continue staining brains with carmine, but cadavers were always hard to come by in Kyoto, because family members never lost any time securing the bodies, and besides there wasn't any carmine. Only in rare, very interesting cases would he acquire the cadaver in question, but then the brain proved boring the minute the diener opened the skull, and so Shimamura would leave the autopsy to his students.

Shimamura was also hesitant to use the animal laboratory, where a bizarre phenomenon could be observed. Cats, rats, guinea pigs, and even reptiles showed such attachment toward Shimamura that experimenting on them was nearly impossible. Even in their anesthetized, poisoned, electrocuted or dissected states the lab animals still courted his favor—they rubbed against him, nibbled at his fingers, clung to his white coat. Once a few students managed to take a photograph of the professor when he was wholly and helplessly covered with frogs. This photo resulted in a number of nicknames, but none of them stuck.

Shimamura displayed thoughtfulness as well as sensitivity in arranging appropriate care and treatment of neurological disorders. Competition was sprouting up everywhere—private asylums (frequently installed near temples and shrines) offered all sorts of strange cures for cash, as though there'd never been a medical reform. They were a thorn in his side and Shimamura railed against them, but even then his little smile got in the way.

The wall mats for which he would become famous originated in 1898. A young mother suffering from delirium as a result of lead poisoning had banged her head against a sharp edge and lost an eye. Medical residents—and not handymen—measured the walls so that everything would be correct, and they also supervised the installation. Shimamura studied the sketches and organized everything. His mind is always with his patients, the students said, but his body prefers to stay at his desk. Nevertheless, after what was arguably his most daring innovation, the introduction of mixed-sex nursing stations, he resumed his bedside visits with some frequency. Now the women were no longer clustered together but well dispersed, and they looked less and less like the love-sick frogs in the animal laboratory.

For nearly two decades Dr. Shimamura spent a great deal of energy concealing the fact that he elicited unusual reactions from his female patients. As a rule he avoided them. He surrounded himself with assistants and stayed in their middle whenever he made his rounds. For examinations he made sure to bring along some distraction: a nurse, family members, children, animals, or he would have a generous dose of narcotics administered in advance.

Only about once a year, and always in summer, would he take a patient into his consulting room and cure her. This he did at night, once everyone was asleep and well past the hour of scheduled treatments, when any noise would be taken for someone shouting in their sleep or for the cries of the insane, and not for the director's howling. Because he inevitably howled—or on occasion, bayed—after he had healed a patient. These nighttime patients did not appear in the health statistics. Shun'ichi Shimamura never recovered.

He had no children and very little interest in public life or amusements, and he spent his free time on numerous interesting pursuits. He studied agrarian science, military affairs, urban planning and traffic control, Noh theater, Nietzsche, the Upanishads, and Italian Baroque painting. After the turn of the century, which caused him a surprising degree of fright, to the point of setting off a fever that kept him chained to his bed for weeks, he began to focus on the ancient Japanese motif of the fox, ultimately acquiring no small expertise.

He studied all the printed material and manuscripts he lugged home from a poorly organized library, and foisted them on his wife to review and copy. Shimamura was convinced that Sachiko was terribly bored, and that drafting abstracts in the service of science suited her better than charity work with insane people. With an austere face Sachiko dutifully catalogued all the representations of the goddess Inari as she appeared in the old manuscripts, and every time she completed a dozen listings she brought them to her husband. As a fox, Inari was as white as snow and had manifold tails. Long ago she had begun her divine life with four tails, and with each century she added a hundred more, so that today, in this sad, late epoch, she sported more tails than human numbers could count. At the same time she always had exactly nine. And at the same time she was also a snake and a spider. She often accompanied herself as her own servant—a winged, single-tailed fox. And at the same time she was a bodhisattva, or even seven, and also water, grain, and land. She was a he as well as an it. "That's going to be a lot of lists, dear," said Sachiko, after she had filled the first fifty pages. Then she lugged the whole pile of documents back to the library all by herself and began a correspondence with the abbot of the Fushimi shrine. He didn't want to hear about foxes so much as donations, and wished someone would send a photographer to take pictures of the shrine for postcards, and at that point Sachiko withdrew from all fox research. She stuck twigs in balls of moss and hung them from the ceiling on invisible threads so that they cast gentle shadows as they dangled.

In 1903 Dr. Shimamura founded a Society for the Study of Myths, which undertook to collect country folk tales about foxes, patterned after the brothers Grimm. Many of his assistants, actually all of them, joined this society, but there was no real enthusiasm. And although it was the last thing he wanted to do, Shimamura wound up traveling across the country, listening to grandmothers tell their fox stories. Even the most ancient women were strangely affected by Shimamura, but nonetheless he managed to collect all kinds of accounts, which he organized by theme, by region, and by the quality of the report. Now and then he told stories himself: about foxes crowned with duckweed who paid homage to the seven stars of the north. About vixens combing their tails against the grain until they sprayed golden sparks. About foxes transformed into will-o-wisps, cedar trees, cotton balls, thresholds. About how ten thousand gods sprang out of a single fox eye. About how Kannon, mother of mercy, one day lost patience with them. Shimamura's favorites were those where a vixen took a human husband, kept his household, bore him children, wove sandals for him, toiled in the rice field and then, once her secret was out, died. He sometimes related that entire protracted tale, and not without emotion. Nicknames again started making the rounds in the Prefectural Medical College, but none of these stuck either.

Over the years he managed to accumulate a handsome collection of woodcuts with fox motifs. Most were depictions of Inari and her court; very few were obscene. No one seemed to care about the collection of tales, which vanished without a trace, but many people were interested in the woodcuts, and especially the Europeans in Kyoto, the so-called honorable foreign guests whose job was to promote modernization. They constantly inquired about the collection. Shimamura hated their visits. Whenever a foreigner came by Shimamura affected a terrible German, excused himself incessantly, and refused to show any print for more than a second. Word soon went around that Professor Shimamura wasn't very nice, and that he was unwilling to sell even the most unremarkable fox print as a souvenir. Ultimately the visits tapered off.

In 1916, for reasons of health, Shun'ichi Shimamura retired from all positions. At the celebrations of his life's work, the tributes, the ceremonies, and the unveiling of his portrait, he mostly let himself be represented by his wife, mother, and mother-in-law, who sat in front like a triumvirate and thanked everyone in his stead.

15

At the beginning of May 1922, when the summer warmth had already set in, Dr. Shimamura received a letter from Tokyo from his old friend and colleague Yoshiro Takaoka, who was coming to Kyoto on business and wanted to visit the doctor in Kameoka.

Shimamura was surprised his wife had simply handed the letter to him instead of tossing it into the waste basket, but this seemed excusable because the letter made no mention of woodcuts or psychiatric mats, and because this Takaoka was an old friend and colleague. Sachiko also gave the impression she was looking forward to the man's visit, so Shimamura wrote back and suggested a date to meet. He had never heard the name Yoshiro Takaoka in his life.

The idea of the visit put him in a foul humor. He was recently feeling a little better, so he decided not to receive Takaoka as a dying man in bed, but rather for afternoon tea. This was a new routine that Sachiko and Hanako had introduced, where everyone sat at a table and chewed odd little cakes Sachiko produced from a prepackaged mix to which she added water to form a kind of dough. Since he had absolutely no recollection who this Takaoka might be, Shimamura decided to wear proper Japanese clothes for the meeting. That would lend a certain formality to the affair, which could in turn shorten it, and besides, it occurred to Shimamura that when it came to receiving old friends, traditional dress could underscore the fact that one was retired and that death was imminent. So he asked the women to search under the floor until they found his good clothes.

Everything had been mothballed and needed to be aired. Shimamura hadn't worn the clothes in years. Sachiko even claimed that it was his wedding garment, but surely she was mistaken. On the day of the visit, long before the afternoon tea, Shimamura locked himself in his room: turning the key inside the lock gave him a deeply satisfying feeling which he resolved to indulge more often in the future. Then he put on his clothes. He did well tying the fine waist knot and also fashioning the jacket cords into a sideways eight, but then everything got tangled. He put both legs in one leg of the hakama, and somehow stuck the jacket inside that. His kimono started coming out of the slits on the side. Then everything hiked up, the long ties slipped down and the hakama became too short, with the cords looped around Shimamura's ankles. Reluctantly he turned the key and called for his wife. Sachiko easily put everything in the right place and tied it off, athough that did not improve Shimamura's mood. But when he examined different parts of himself in his shaving mirror, he approved of what his brain pieced together: he looked like the ghost of a tubercular samurai. In the house of someone like that no one drank tea longer than absolutely necessary. Shimamura had to laugh. Even Sachiko had to laugh. Shimamura paced up and down inside the house, constantly emitting the cool, coarse rustle that a good thick silk hakama makes with every step. "Oh, oh!" said Yukiko. Sachiko started mixing her dough and sent the housemaid on some errands so she wouldn't be singing in the garden later on. After that there was nothing to do but wait.

Yoshiro Takaoka and his wife arrived in a petrol-blue Chevrolet, which lumbered and rattled down the poor street, pursued by all the children in Kameoka. Shimamura and his wife stood in the entrance to their house and watched as Takaoka parked the car behind the quince trees and cautioned the children not to damage it in any way. In the meantime his wife took off a series of scarves that had kept her hat in place during the trip. Yoshiro Takaoka wore a leather cap like the pilot of an aeroplane. He seemed to be fighting the desire to clean the dust from the trip off his Chevrolet, ideally for hours. Then he took off his cap and with his wife walked up the pathway. Both were at least fifty but were dressed like a young couple out of an American magazine.

The Shimamuras greeted the Takaokas and the Takaokas greeted the Shimamuras. They exchanged polite talk, about the weather, the quinces, the Chevrolet, and the passage of time. Then the guests went inside the house. Dr. Shimamura rustled. Sachiko made compliments. Hanako and Yukiko were introduced but quickly and regretfully excused themselves—Shimamura had explained in advance that his nerves couldn't withstand four women at the table simultaneously. The Takaokas were given water to wash their hands. They talked about sunlight, dust, automobiles and this beautiful house. Then Sachiko invited the guests to tea. Takaoka's wife was also familiar with the magical mixture that produced the little cakes. She had large toes, no longer young, possibly rheumatic, which could be seen clearly through her silk stockings, she showed beautiful teeth when she laughed, and one strand of hair that dangled from under her hat had been curled into a spiral. With a solemn rustle Shimamura pulled back his hakama so he could spread out comfortably as he sat down. And then there was tea. Shun'ichi Shimamura had never seen Yoshiro Takaoka before in his entire life.

Takaoka held a high position in the Tokyo municipal administration. His hobby was an automobile magazine called Speed, for which he wrote reports and technical notes and frequently also took pictures. This was the reason for the Chevrolet and the couple's youthful get-up, for which they both somewhat apologized. Naturally they continued to talk about time—how long it had been, how fleeting and fast-paced life was, how relentlessly it went by. The Shimamuras learned that the idea of establishing June 10th as a national holiday honoring time stemmed from Takaoka himself. This Time Day, which was observed with sweets and paper decorations in the form of clocks and was above all a celebration of punctuality in professional life, had existed officially for two years, but in their seclusion it had escaped the Shimamuras. Takaoka seemed very proud of his holiday. He started to launch into a longer description, but his wife, with a gentle mocking, interrupted him. Then Takaoka felt obliged to joke about everything that had gone wrong in his life. Evidently they had a wayward son who was trying his luck in motion pictures, and then there was Takaoka's study of medicine. "You taught me so much," said he said to Shimamura, "but I was too dumb and too muddleheaded for this honorable profession, so I became an economist."

"That's the way things go in life," said Shimamura. "Ah yes. The economy."

"Ah yes," said Sachiko.

"Well now," sighed Takaoka.

"Do you still remember me?" asked his wife. "You saved my life. With your medical art and quinine. Malaria. You remember, don't you, Doctor, in Shimane, back then, that summer, it was so long ago, wasn't it?"

"Ah yes," mouthed Shimamura. "Of course. Oh life, life."

"Ah yes?" asked Sachiko.

Shimamura didn't know what to do. He stared, practically agog, first at Takaoka's wife and then at Takaoka.

"My wife was a patient," said Takaoka to Sachiko, "and I was a student, and we eloped, as they say, we eloped and married in secret, without any family. Afterwards everything was a complete mess, we lived like a bunch of acrobats – anyway we were young and I'm sure you wouldn't want to hear all the details."

"No, I'm sure she wouldn't," said his wife. She covered her face with her hands as though she was terribly ashamed, but in actuality she was giggling.

"Ah, students," said Sachiko, smiling.

"Malaria?" mumbled Shimamura.

"It still pains me enormously that I didn't keep in touch," said Yoshiro Takaoka. Then he reached across the table, all the way across the entire table, pulled Shimamura's right hand out of its sleeve and squeezed it with his own.

For a moment even Sachiko lost her composure. She stood up to fetch more cakes—some different, better ones—along with some lemonade since it was so warm, and also so she could regain her composure in the kitchen. How ill-mannered these Tokyoites were, what with grabbing hands and that Chevrolet!

"Kiyo," said Shimamura. "I didn't expect to see you so again doing so well."

"I was such a dumb kid," said Takaoka.

"That terrible fever," said his wife.

Then they all shook their heads.

Sachiko returned and Takaoka talked and talked and Kiyo smiled, laughed, and Shimamura still didn't recognize them. Only bit by bit did the old pictures come into focus: Takaoka in the rickshaw. Takaoka in the inn. Takaoka by the miserable sickbed. Young Takaoka with his camera and his bare bottom, the way he talked, talked, talked. All of a sudden Shimamura laughed out loud. "Do you remember, you chatterbox," he asked cheerfully, "do you remember when we were young— the foxes?"

"The foxes!" Yoshiro Takaoka said gleefully.

"Oh, the foxes!" Kiyo Takaoka shouted. "Oh yes! We all had the fox back then, all the girls, every summer, in Shimane over the sea!"

And then they laughed some more and drank lemonade.

The Takaokas enjoyed the afternoon, and somehow the Shimamuras also appreciated the change of pace. They walked a bit in the garden, talked about quinces and flowers. Shimamura regretted his choice of clothing; it was silly to act so formal in his own home. The children of Kameoka, who were still besieging the Chevrolet, pointed at him in secret. The hard silk pin-stripes creaked and crackled in the short grass.

Little by little Shimamura began to recognize Takaoka better and better. More than three decades had passed: he couldn't be blamed for no longer being a strapping youth. Also Kiyo became more recognizable once her old toes disappeared in the cream-colored lace shoes, and her curled hair was glowing in the sunlight. But Shimamura didn't know whether he was remembering the girl from Shimane in this woman or perhaps all the girls, all the girlhoods long since past. "Ach" said Shimamura. He smoked Takaoka's American cigarettes, which did his bronchia an amazing amount of good.

"Who was that?" Shun'ichi Shimamura asked his wife, after the guests had gone and he could finally undress.

"Dear?"

"Who that was, please, Sachiko!" He seldom called her by her name.

Sachiko smiled. Shimamura wrinkled his forehead. Sachiko glided out of the room. Shimamura knew she was lurking behind the door. She would end up folding the damned hakama for him after he had tried ten times and given up. The sun went down. What a long day.

"All my memories," Dr. Shimamura wrote that night in his notebook, "come from Josef Breuer's chaise longue on the Brandstätte in Vienna." Then he took his notebook and all the other notebooks, as well as all the notes and jottings that contained plans for his book on memory, carried them into the kitchen, stoked the fire and shoved everything inside. That was Sachiko's fault. Why, he didn't know.

16

July came, August, then an early September autumn, and Shun'ichi Shimamura did not die. He felt stronger, breathed more easily, slept better, and his fever vacillated between 99 and 100 degrees Fahrenheit. Every four days he still treated himself to a scopolamine injection, but that had become a luxury he could scarcely enjoy, as his dreams became increasingly boring, nothing more than random sexual fiddle-faddle.

In the middle of September he removed the fern that had been in the small urn next to his desk. The plant had likely been dead for weeks; it had no roots and was lying loose and lopsided across the soil.

At the end of September the left sleeve of his housecoat tore off for no apparent reason. It slid off his hand and dropped to the floor. Shimamura examined the sleeve and saw that over the years all the fleurs-de-lis had been worn sheer, nothing was left but a few brittle threads. He discovered the entire robe was in this condition. With great regret and after long hesitation he threw it away.

Now he often wrapped himself in a quilted blanket and sat on the porch in a folding chair, reading the newspaper. The women kept on about their business; they came and went, at times barely paying him any attention. For Shimamura that was the primary indication that his death was no longer so imminent.

Yukiko was displaying signs of senile dementia. Sometimes when she went to the temple she couldn't find her way back and had to be escorted home by a neighbor or a child. She also ranted a lot. Although she had gone decades without ever mentioning it, she complained incessantly about her sore hip, which she blamed on everyone else. She was of no real use in the household. Sachiko assigned her small tasks, to keep her from yammering, but Yukiko was incapable of finishing anything, she dropped whatever she picked up, and kept asking why Sachiko had to marry this man who did nothing but sit around. "I ask myself that question," Sachiko said, smiling, "but Father will know the answer." Whenever Yukiko came onto the porch Shimamura went straight to his room.

Hanako, sprightly as ever, watched over Yukiko every night and slapped her gently when her breathing faltered. She had long since given up on her son's biography, and since she hadn't found any other occupation, the nights were very long and boring.

The housemaid still brought a bucket of water into Dr. Shimamura's room every morning. In December, after he finally gave up the scopolamine altogether, every fourth day he treated himself to a conversation with the maid. Shimamura had her sit down in the rattan armchair and would then tell her something, sometimes in Japanese, sometimes in German and mostly half-and-half. He told her about the Suez Canal, the pink tongues of the ladies' little dogs in the Place de l'Étoile. He told her about Dr. Bidet's reaction times. About Josef Breuer who kept opening the window in his consulting room and about Barbara the landlady's daughter who was insulted. Occasionally, when he didn't know what else to say, he pulled the tattered Griesinger off the shelf and read a passage out loud. *Where the disorder principally shows itself in evil desires, eccentricities, perverseness of every kind, the intelligence being well-preserved, the disease showing itself far more by senseless actions than by insane thoughts and speech ... the patients perform foolish actions and show perversity of demeanor, but are also in a position to justify and to explain their conduct by a course of coherent reasoning which still lies within the bounds of possibility, i.e. folie raisonnante.* How outmoded he sounded, Dr. Griesinger with his weak chin! Shimamura stood up and looked down at the housemaid. For some time her breasts had been well contained. Perhaps Sachiko had given her a so-called brassiere. "This is an impolite question," said Shimamura, "but tell me one thing, Luise: what is about me that you find so endearing?" And then he went on talking because he had long since given up expecting an answer.

The maid rose from the chair. She locked her knees, put her hands together and straightened her head. And then she began to scream: "Not endearing!" Her voice came from deep inside her stomach, then rose high into her head and turned into a tantrum, a screech. "Not endearing! No!" she screamed. She kicked over the bucket. Shimamura was stunned. She swept everything off the desk. She hurled the Griesinger through the window paper and flung a paperweight against the European door. She stamped her foot. The sodden oriental rug squished and squirted. "Not endearing!" she screamed, screeched, sang, trilled. When the futon's down feathers started flying Shimamura made his escape. He removed the key and put it back in the lock from the outside, then gave it two turns. But Sei smashed through the outer wall, evidently with her bare hands, and continued her raving on the porch. She kicked over the railing; even part of the roof collapsed. Holding the rattan chair in both arms she dashed around the house and came back in through the main entrance, still screaming. She plowed into the wardrobe and knocked it over along with two large vases. Finally Sachiko took a piece of wood and knocked the raving woman to the ground. When Sei woke up she was calm. She apologized, once, very curtly and with clenched teeth. She didn't resist when they took her to Kyoto, where she lived for many years in the Prefectural University Neurological Clinic, and soon no one remembered her name and whether she was a nurse or a patient.

At the beginning of March 1923, after one more snow, Shun'ichi Shimamura spotted a fox for the very first time. It was twilight and the fox was standing still under the quince trees. It was a vixen carrying a cub in her mouth. The weak light from the house lit up her eyes. Shimamura crouched down and the animal bolted. But then it stopped for a moment and looked back, as if to say: one never knows.

The next morning Dr. Shimamura felt so much recovered that he discarded his diagnosis of consumption. He called the women together. The mood was festive. Eight days later he had a stroke and died in his sleep.

New Directions Paperbooks — a partial listing

Javier Marías, Your Face Tomorrow (3 volumes)
Harry Mathews, The Solitary Twin
Bernadette Mayer, Works & Days
Carson McCullers, The Member of the Wedding
Thomas Merton, New Seeds of Contemplation
  The Way of Chuang Tzu
Henri Michaux, A Barbarian in Asia
Dunya Mikhail, The Beekeeper
Henry Miller, The Colossus of Maroussi
  Big Sur & the Oranges of Hieronymus Bosch
Yukio Mishima, Confessions of a Mask
  Death in Midsummer
Eugenio Montale, Selected Poems*
Vladimir Nabokov, Laughter in the Dark
  Nikolai Gogol
  The Real Life of Sebastian Knight
Raduan Nassar, A Cup of Rage
Pablo Neruda, The Captain's Verses*
  Love Poems*
  Residence on
Charles Olson, Selected Writings
George Oppen, New Collected Poems
Wilfred Owen, Collected Poems
Michael Palmer, The Laughter of the Sphinx
Nicanor Parra, Antipoems*
Boris Pasternak, Safe Conduct
Kenneth Patchen
  Memoirs of a Shy Pornographer
Octavio Paz, Poems of Octavio Paz
Victor Pelevin, Omon Ra
Alejandra Pizarnik
  Extracting the Stone of Madness
Ezra Pound, The Cantos
  New Selected Poems and Translations
Raymond Queneau, Exercises in Style
Qian Zhongshu, Fortress Besieged
Raja Rao, Kanthapura
Herbert Read, The Green Child
Kenneth Rexroth, Selected Poems
Keith Ridgway, Hawthorn & Child
Rainer Maria Rilke
  Poems from the Book of Hours
Arthur Rimbaud, Illuminations*
  A Season in Hell and The Drunken Boat*
Guillermo Rosales, The Halfway House
Evelio Rosero, The Armies
Fran Ross, Oreo
Joseph Roth, The Emperor's Tomb
  The Hotel Years

Raymond Roussel, Locus Solus
Ihara Saikaku, The Life of an Amorous Woman
Nathalie Sarraute, Tropisms
Jean-Paul Sartre, Nausea
  The Wall
Delmore Schwartz
  In Dreams Begin Responsibilities
Hasan Shah, The Dancing Girl
W. G. Sebald, The Emigrants
  The Rings of Saturn
  Vertigo
Stevie Smith, Best Poems
Gary Snyder, Turtle Island
Muriel Spark, The Driver's Seat
  The Girls of Slender Means
  Memento Mori
Reiner Stach, Is That Kafka?
Antonio Tabucchi, Pereira Maintains
Junichiro Tanizaki, A Cat, a Man & Two Women
Yoko Tawada, The Emissary
  Memoirs of a Polar Bear
Dylan Thomas, A Child's Christmas in Wales
  Collected Poems
Uwe Timm, The Invention of Curried Sausage
Tomas Tranströmer
  The Great Enigma: New Collected Poems
Leonid Tsypkin, Summer in Baden-Baden
Tu Fu, Selected Poems
Frederic Tuten, The Adventures of Mao
Regina Ullmann, The Country Road
Paul Valéry, Selected Writings
Enrique Vila-Matas, Bartleby & Co.
  Vampire in Love
Elio Vittorini, Conversations in Sicily
Rosmarie Waldrop, Gap Gardening
Robert Walser, The Assistant
  Microscripts
  The Tanners
Eliot Weinberger, The Ghosts of Birds
Nathanael West, The Day of the Locust
  Miss Lonelyhearts
Tennessee Williams, Cat on a Hot Tin Roof
  The Glass Menagerie
  A Streetcar Named Desire
William Carlos Williams, Selected Poems
  Spring and All
Mushtaq Ahmed Yousufi, Mirages of the Mind
Louis Zukofsky, "A"
  Anew

*BILINGUAL EDITION

For a complete listing, request a free catalog from New Directions, 80 8th Avenue, New York, NY 10011 or visit us online at **ndbooks.com**